DEEP BREATH

JASON

HOLD TIGHT

GURLEY

Deep Breath Hold Tight:
Stories About the End of Everything
Jason Gurley

Copyright © 2014 Jason Gurley
www.jasongurley.com

Novels

Greatfall
The Settlers
The Colonists
The Man Who Ended the World

Short Stories

The Last Rail-Rider
The Book of Matthew (The End of Greatfall)
The Caretaker
The Dark Age
Wolf Skin

DEEP

BREATH

HOLD

TIGHT

For Janice Gruhn

CONTENTS

WOLF SKIN

Cutting a person's throat is not as easy as I thought it would be.

I remember the old movies — rich and colorful distractions from the days none of us knew were coming. In the movies, the villain draws a blade over a person's throat like a marker, and the throat opens like a peach, juicy and bright. Maybe in the movies their knives were sharper than real ones. The movies don't tell you that skin makes a sound when it tears, that you have to put shoulders and weight into the cutting — that the cutting is not an easy thing, but that you have to *saw*.

The movies don't teach you which way to lean to avoid the spray of blood. They don't tell you that blood is hot, that it stinks of sour copper.

They don't teach you that a person fights to their

final breath, kicking and squirming in a fountain of red, that their breath turns pink like winter mist.

They don't tell you that sometimes the person stares at you with eyes so wide that it's as if their lids have been cut away, their pupils wide to drink in all of their last light. They fix on you, stare at you. You're the last thing they see, until their eyes wander, their focus lost, and they stop struggling. They twitch like dead birds, little last muscle spasms turning them into grotesque, dancing marionettes.

There isn't supposed to be time to notice such things. In my world, you're expected to cut the throat and move on. There are more of them to catch, more necks to saw open. Only the men, though. If you're fortunate enough to catch a woman or a child, you leave their necks alone.

"Take a hand from the women," Grant said during my first raid. "They'll be grateful you didn't take more."

From the children, he explained, you take nothing. They will need their hands and their strength. You leave their bodies alone.

"Make them hold their mother's arm when you take her hand," he said. "Let them cling to their father when you open his neck."

That was how you built an army these days.

So said Grant.

I remember video games.

Loud, vibrant worlds filled with the staccato thumping of gunfire. The rush of voices in your ear — other players, somewhere else in the world, calling you terrible names. In some of those games, cutting a person's throat was as easy as pulling a plastic trigger, as tapping a little green button. Entire populations could be vanished into history with presses of little buttons.

These days you have to take them apart person by person.

In the last of days, the games were almost real themselves. You could walk a character into an open field and stand there quietly, and just look around and appreciate beauty. Rendered forests rose up into perfect blue skies. Sun filtered through the branches in lazy beams. Flares of light washed out your vision if you looked at it too closely. The hum of cicadas would swell up to fill your character's silence. You could hear your own footsteps, different each time, crunching on cold winter grass or squelching in mud. The occasional bird flapped overhead, silent but for the shadow it cast on the ground at your feet.

At night I dream of video games, of those worlds. I dream in greens and blues and pinks.

When I open my eyes each morning, I see browns and grays. The world I see is only a memory of my childhood. The land is infertile and dry, the mountains cracked and flaking away like brittle scabs on the earth. Every river runs black and slow, or has long ago dried. I haven't seen a living animal in months. The skies are thick like sand, the sun just a dim glow behind toxic clouds.

The weapons I hold are nothing like the games. Strapped to my hip is a pistol, but the spinner-thing falls out sometime. I don't fire it because I'm certain it will explode, and I'll lose a hand like the women who walk the rope line. My knife is short and dented and flecked with rust, and hasn't been sharp since before I found it stuck in a fencepost.

I look down at my hands. They used to hold those video game controllers. They used to be pale and a little soft. Now the dirt has been driven so deep into my pores that my skin is mottled and dark. My fingernails are caked with black. Old blood has stained my skin the color of rust. It's hard to tell which blood is mine.

The bright days of my memory are recent enough that I still sometimes wake from sleep into them. It doesn't seem possible, once my head clears, but for a moment I still hear the sounds of my father busying himself in the kitchen, of my mother starting the car and leaving for work.

~⊚~

I didn't know why Grant needed an army.

I wouldn't consider our bunch to be anything like an army at all. We were like a pack of wolves, moving over the land in a broken line, drawing blood from anything that opposed us. We took what we could, and sometimes we killed for things only to drop them hours later, tired of carrying them.

Armies usually fight other armies, but what we did was horrifying. We would find a camp, or a little town, and we would separate into small knots and hunt. "Look for lights," Grant always said. "Lights mean life."

So we did. There wasn't electricity anymore, but if we saw electric light it almost certainly meant we were going to find a stockpile. Some man with a shotgun and a thousand rounds, hunkered down in a house with a generator and enough canned food for a year. Guys like that were easy — they almost always shot themselves after realizing we were going to get in one way or another.

Mostly we saw campfires. We raided in the middle of the night. Fires were easy to spot, even if they were dying down to embers. And all of the old battle tropes held true, I guess. Grant always said the best time to stage an attack was four o'clock in the morning, just before the sun came up, when the night watches got lazy and before the sleeping soldiers began to stir. That's what we did, and he was right, mostly.

Except these weren't soldiers. They were never soldiers.

∼౭∽

Looking back I think what surprises me most is that the change happened so quickly. Within weeks of the first bombs, the sky had turned the color of dull rust, and people began to wear masks to filter out the fine black debris. The masks turned black, too. Not every town was hit, but every town came apart like a flimsy paper castle. It was dark all the time, almost, and the dark brings out the worst in a person. Ordinary people started looting and panicking. They kicked in their neighbors' doors and stole what they could, and took by force what they had to. Insurance agents were shot down in their yards by bank tellers. Church folk really lost their shit, especially the ones who were convinced that Jesus had come back and forgotten all about them.

People turned into animals practically overnight.

They forgot what it felt like to sit down at a table for dinner, forgot the calm heat of a drawn bath. They forgot about things like shaking hands or saying hello. Before too long, if you were to see another person out in the open, you learned you were safest if you considered that person an enemy, and shot them down first. Only one thing mattered: yourself.

I remember the first time I saw a pack like ours.

I had found myself an apartment in a cluttered complex in a destitute part of my hometown. It made sense to me, an apartment. There was only one way in, one way out. I could barricade the door and stay relatively safe, and that's what I did. I pushed the dead refrigerator and a china cabinet in front of the door, and unhooked the washing machine — it was one of those double-stacked units with a dryer built-in — and hefted that into place, too. I figured that somebody could probably get in with enough leverage. But the apartment door faced a narrow walkway that was seven levels up. It was three feet from the door to the wrought-iron railing. Not enough room to get enough guys in there to push hard.

Every day or two, I heard the sounds of doors being kicked in all over the apartment complex. Sometimes they'd get to mine, and I'd hear someone kick really hard, and I'd see the refrigerator jolt a fraction of an inch, and maybe they'd kick again. But they always gave up.

In the little bathroom there was a window that looked down over the lawn and the street behind the apartments. I kept the window closed, even though the apartment had grown stuffy in the heat. I had seen someone down there throwing rocks at the building. The rocks were wrapped in knotted rags, and they were burning. I didn't think anybody could hit the small bathroom window, much less throw something through the window from so far down — but why take chances? Better to be sweaty and uncomfortable than to be smoked out into the open.

There were screams all the time at first. I could hear them at night when I slept, could hear them during the day when I huddled in the apartment. I saw a woman raped in the middle of the street, and I watched from the bathroom window as someone came to her aid and pummeled her attacker with a baseball bat. Then the rescuer beat the woman to death, too, and ran away, nothing gained or lost by the encounter.

That was how quickly the world had changed.

I lived in the apartment for three weeks, rationing what little food was already inside, and the little I'd brought in my pack. The former occupant must have been at work when things went down, or I'd have had to fight them for the apartment for sure. I thought about them sometimes. There were photos on the bookcase in the apartment's lone bedroom — pictures of families and groups of people. The one constant in the photos was a man with dark hair and thick glasses. I guessed that this was his apartment. I found a stack of paid bills on the kitchen counter, all addressed to Kevin J. Francoeur.

Before long I was talking to the guy. I didn't even notice at first, but maybe in retrospect it was better than talking to myself.

Kev had a thing for Campbell's soup, for which I was grateful. The apartment pantry was well-stocked with the stuff — mostly chicken and stars. Not chicken noodle, but chicken and star-shaped pasta. Kev had a big-kid streak running through him. But there were other ones, too — ham and beans, chunky beef and vegetables. I sawed them open with a bent can opener I found in a drawer, and sipped from them, rationing them out over the course of two days each.

I got used to the growling of my stomach.

There was all kinds of food in the refrigerator, mostly frozen stuff, but without electricity or gas, I couldn't prepare any of it, and I certainly couldn't save it. I waited for nightfall and opened the bathroom window and one by one pushed the frozen Hungry Man dinners out into the dark and listened to them clatter like heavy books to the ground below.

I was in the middle of doing this one night when I first saw the marauders. They were just shadows, but my eyes were well-adjusted to the night. I had no light in the apartment. I stopped dropping food out of the window and ducked, even though at this height I didn't think I was visible. I cranked the window shut quietly, and after a few minutes I peeked out again.

They were like panthers in the dark, slinking between cars and through trees and over fences. I watched a few of them band together here and there and kick their way into the darkened old houses. Mostly they came out empty-handed. Most of the people had long fled, or been killed and robbed already.

I was terrified by the sight of a man creeping over the apartment lawn, his neck clearly craned upward as he studied the windows. I leaned away from the glass, and when I looked back down he was standing directly below my window, seven stories down, kicking at the frozen dinners. He picked one up and shook it, then stepped back several yards and stood there in the dark, staring up. I didn't dare move — I thought that if I moved he might see me, and if I didn't, he might mistake me for a shadow or a curtain.

He moved on, dropping the box and rejoining his partners, and they disappeared down the street. I heard someone's car alarm cry out a few minutes later, and then I heard gunshots, and then the night was quiet again.

I couldn't sleep that night. I knew that the world had changed, and that the odds were incredibly high that one day, men like that would find me and that would be that.

And that happened, eventually.

Except they didn't kill me.

They kept me.

❧

I've been a part of Grant's gang for — I don't even know how long. Years. I remember that I was twenty years old when I holed up in that apartment. I was a college student — on the verge of dropping out, if I'm honest — and I worked in the campus bookstore for a few bucks. I was lean then, and I'm leaner now, but somewhere along the way the shape of my bones changed. My shoulders broadened, my neck stretched. I am taller, and wider, and from time to time when I catch a glimpse of myself in a window that hasn't already been busted-out, I stop and stare at the Neanderthal I have become. I have a beard — everyone in the clan has beards — that has grown thick and long. It crawls up my face towards my eyes, and its weight draws it down in a heavy hank. My hair is long and tangled. I only have one of my ears. A young father bit the other off when I helped Grant and two other men take his wife and his daughter away from him. Grant showed me how to open the man's belly just so, and I watched the man stare at his own insides spilling onto the cabin floor.

Ten years, at least. Maybe more. Which would put me at thirty. Had I followed my parents' path, by thirty I should have been a father myself, with a couple of little ones and a wife and a small, probably rented house. I'd be working as a teacher, or a tech support manager, or something like that. I'd come home to my kind wife and well-behaved kids.

And then someone would take them from me and pour my guts out in front of me.

I have seen more death than my father ever did. He skipped Vietnam by marrying my mother and having me. I think sometimes of his own father, Grandpa Mickey, who fought in Europe. I sometimes think that Grandpa Mickey and I might have something in common now. He'd always thought of me as gentle and soft, the kind of child who lived in books and movies and video games, who took a punch from a bully and didn't swing back, who maybe still wet the bed.

Grandpa Mickey would be terrified of me now.

When we raid a town, Grant lets us take whatever we want, so long as we can carry it without dragging down the clan. Over the years we've accumulated a lot of things, and a lot of ways to carry them. Our clan moves more slowly now than it once did. We used to run on foot like warriors, old blades hanging from our shoulders, pistols on our hips, stuffed into pockets. We were comparatively small then, maybe fifty or sixty strong.

There are four hundred or more of us now. Most

are hunters and raiders like me, the workhorses of the clan. We're dirty and we smell like sweat and blood and we bunk down in groups every evening, sometimes in abandoned houses, sometimes in the open. We carry tents. Grant has one of his own, and five or six of the women share it with him at night. We have animals — a few tired old mules, a horse or two — and they pull old flat wagons piled high with our things. One of the men has learned how to siphon gas from the underground reservoirs, and so a pair of old flatbed work trucks follows in our wake, gear lashed in place. Most of it is food stores we've stolen along the way. Not that there's much food after all this time.

We pick up domesticated animals when we find them, and tie them to the truck rails. They plod along beside for as long as they can, and when they fall over, they become rations for the men. Skinny old cows, shaggy sheep with dirty, matted wool. Sometimes dogs that have gone feral.

You do what you have to these days.

∽⊚∾

When I was fourteen, my high school drama class took a field trip to Los Angeles. Our instructor was friends with a woman who worked at Warner Brothers, and she had arranged a backlot tour for us. We wandered fake studio streets, stared up at familiar two-dimensional facades. The water tower with the WB logo loomed overhead. It reminded me of cartoons. We saw classic old cars — the orange General Lee, the psychedelic Mystery Machine.

My father had been reluctant to sign the permission slip. Mom and I had pressed him. She was convinced that he was resentful of my "soft" upbringing, my interest in the arts. I had a feeling it was something else — Dad and I had wonderful conversations about movies sometimes, and I don't think he resented me for loving anything. I think he resented himself for never allowing himself to.

But it turned out to be something entirely different. Dad had friends in L.A., old war buddies, who told him that parts of the city were practically a war zone. They told him about gang violence, and shootings, and about the underbelly of the Hollywood experience. Dad was afraid of seeing my dreams torn open by the craggy reality of the city.

He relented, and I went, and I didn't join any gangs, and no Hollywood actors offered me baggies of cocaine or tried to sell me into sex slavery. I didn't see anybody famous, unless you counted Tom Arnold. Our instructor had to explain who Arnold was. None of us had ever seen his work before.

I was quite safe, as it all turned out, and I returned home glowing from the trip. I'd seen behind the curtain, and Hollywood, I found, was wholesome and creative, and it was going to be my future.

Dad would weep for me now, I think.

I don't have any illusions anymore.

჻

Grant tested me, as I later learned he tested all new recruits. He promised me food and a blanket, and told me that if I did well, then one day I might have a tent of my own, and a woman to share it with me. He would pick a good one, he said. I didn't know if he was talking about the tent or the woman.

We broke over a town called Waterton like a thin but angry wave. Grant ran alongside me that day, and taught me how to kick open a door just right. It didn't always work, so he also showed me how to break a window without slicing my arm to ribbons.

"Always carry a coat," he said, wrapping it around his elbow.

He punched out the window and cleared the loose glass from the frame, then stepped back and gestured sweepingly, like a butler inviting me inside a palace.

The house was dark, as all of them were, and stank of sour milk and bad food and shit. I heard a scrabbling noise, and saw a small dog, nothing but hair and bones and nails, weakly run up the stairs. The kitchen was piled high with dishes, the pantry emptied, torn boxes and plastic strewn everywhere. There wasn't a shred of food in sight.

Grant came in after me. "They'll be upstairs, if they're still here," he said.

I pointed at a door beneath the staircase. "Not the basement?"

He shook his head. "Basements scare people," he said. "Nobody willingly sits in a dark basement for any reason at all. Too much they can't see. Bugs and nightmares are worse than we are."

And he was right. We didn't go in the basement. We found a skinny man and woman shivering with fear in a small closet. They had pulled clothes from hangers to cover themselves up.

"Get em out," Grant said.

They kicked and swatted at me as I pulled the clothes off of them.

"Don't touch her," the man said, his voice weak and old-sounding. "Leave her alone, leave her alone."

"They always say that," Grant said, bored.

I didn't know what I was supposed to feel. They weren't very old, maybe just six or seven years older than I was. Not yet thirty, still so much of their life ahead of them, at least before the wars. The man had watery green eyes, and was probably handsome once. The woman was plain but pretty, even with her knotted, frizzy hair like pulled cotton. In the old days, the days *before*, they could have been teachers. They might have been churchgoers. They probably owned a respectable, responsible car with four doors, in case they decided to have children.

"They're already ghosts," Grant said.

❧

That was how he explained it, when he was feeling generous, or drunk. The clan wasn't a band of vicious marauders, pillaging and taking for itself whatever it wanted, but a merciful battalion of angels, bringing an ending to people whose lives had continued on long after their souls had withered. He described the starving people we found as *husks*, as *ghosts*, as memories of the people they used to be.

"I was a mechanic," he told me once. "Before. But look at me now. Doing the good Lord's work, don't you think?"

My family didn't go to church, and I didn't know much about gods, but I knew enough to think that Jesus probably didn't want people like Grant killing his kids. But I wanted to eat, and I wanted a tent and a blanket on the cold, dumb nights, and I wanted Grant to give me a woman who would do whatever I told her to, and keep me from feeling the sting of every single day, the dread of every day that was lined up behind it, heavy and ready to fall on me, one domino after the next.

⤙֎⤚

He made me hold the man, and he took the woman's hand himself. She was too weak to get away. He laid her arm across a dresser, and splayed her hand flat. Her fingers reflexively curled inward again, and he leaned on the back of her hand with the knob of his elbow, and she cried out, and I felt the man try to surge forward, but it was easy to hold him back. He was flamingo-thin and hungry and had nothing inside of him, no fuel, no real fire.

"Flat," Grant said to the woman, and she opened

her fingers slowly. She sobbed, and I could see her bright pink skin in the wake of her tears.

"Maybe —" I started, and Grant turned, and stared at me, hard.

"Maybe what?" he asked. He looked at the woman, then the man, then at me. "Maybe let her be? Maybe let him live?"

I swallowed hard and looked away.

"You know better," he said. He wasn't angry, just stern. He pulled a fish knife from a sleeve on his belt, and the woman jerked, and so did the man. Grant pointed the knife at her face and said, "You be still. Consider this your admission into the afterlife. Your ticket to a life with purpose. Doing the Lord's work for those doing the Lord's work. Understand?"

"Leave her alone," the man grunted again.

Grant sighed. "Say a couple of prayers," he told the man patiently. "She's going to get through this. But you won't."

"Does he have to watch?" I asked.

Grant opened his mouth to argue, then closed it. "Genius," he said to me. He turned the fish knife over and held it out to me, the blade loosely pinched between his dirty fingers. "She can watch instead."

I stared at the butt of the knife, and the man struggled in my arms like a dog that doesn't want a bath.

"Go on," Grant said.

It was my first kill. I held the knife in my hand, and for a long moment I stared at the woman, her red, pleading eyes, her quivering mouth. A million thoughts ran through my head, and all seemed to lead to one stupid idea: *I could kill Grant. I could save these two.*

But it wouldn't work. I couldn't see how to make it work. And the clan had warm food and blankets.

"It's never easy the first time," Grant said, his voice almost warm. "He's a ghost already. It's humane. It's kind."

I tightened my arm around the man's neck and lifted the knife. Grant told me where to put the blade, and when I had it right, he told me to cut. The woman screamed herself hoarse, and Grant stomped on her foot, and she slid down the dresser to the floor like a doll. She tried to crawl in my direction, but Grant's boot was heavy, and he leaned all of his weight onto her foot, and she cried like a child.

He nodded at me, and I closed my eyes and swiped the knife across the man's throat. The man screamed and I heard the wet sound of him pissing himself.

"Not like that," Grant said.

I opened my eyes and looked down, then at the dresser. In the mounted mirror there, I could see the man struggling in my arms, his grimy neck exposed. There was a perforated line on his skin, with little beads of blood welling up.

That's when Grant told me how you had to play a man's neck like a violin, how to grip the knife handle at a certain angle, how to dig the blade in, slightly upward, to make the first cut easier, and how to draw it hard and fast and deep.

"But point him that way," he said, finally, and I did,

and as the woman's exhausted cries filled the room, as the man limply struggled in my grasp, I listened to Grant's instructions, and I opened the man's throat, and all I saw was red. I felt his hands fall away from my arm immediately, felt them flapping around, felt his fear fall over the room like a black cloak. I could tell when he died, because he fell silent and still, and the blood stopped pumping, and began to just leak out of him.

"Let go," Grant said.

I did, and the man fell to the floor like a *thing*, not like a man, and he sagged onto his side and the rest of him bled onto the wood floor. I stared at him, his dirty skin growing pale almost quickly enough for me to see it happening.

I felt the knife slick in my hands, felt the sudden wet heaviness of my own clothes, and realized that I was drenched in a stranger's blood. The smell was overpowering, and I threw up, and bent over and coughed up everything that was inside of me.

Behind me I heard a heavy *thock*, and a choked scream, and then a ripping sound as Grant shredded a bed sheet for a tourniquet.

Then he said, "Alright, let's go, boy," and I stepped over the spreading black blood and followed him down the stairs. He opened the door and we left like respectable people. The last thing I heard was the click-click of tiny nails on hardwood, then a terrible, small lapping sound from the nightmarish bedroom.

And then I was one of them.

Grant gave me a tent. "Yours for a few days," he

said.

I hammered the pegs into the ground, and while the rest of the clan slept on the damp earth that night, I crawled into the relative darkness of the tent, and all night long I stared up at the fraying plastic sheet above me.

One of them.

A wolf.

⌒◎⌒

In every town we stole things. Most men wanted the women, and fought over them, and some wanted the children, and Grant made a new rule: He who took the woman's hand could have her, but only for a few days, like a tent, and then she would become common clan property, passed around and made to work. The women were tied together by their good hands and forced to walk behind the trucks, tired and dirty and lifeless, the fight and color gone from them.

After I killed my first man, I stopped wanting my own woman. Every time I looked at one of them, I heard the horror of their screams, saw the men who died to protect them. Every man who failed lived on in their haunted eyes.

Instead, I stole books. I didn't read much before the wars, unless I had to. I lived for movies. Video games didn't make you read books. But in the dark days there was no electricity. I dreamed of movies, and they lived on in my memory like old reels, slowly coming apart over the years.

So for me it was books. I read anything I could find, and when I was done, I would put the book on the truck for someone else, and steal another from the next town. It took a long time to realize that nobody else gave a shit about them, and my collection of books grew large.

Grant dumped them off between towns one day.

"Not a damn library," he said.

The others started calling me Librarian, and my habit made me different, and different was unpleasant. I slept at distance from the others. If they bunked in a house, I slept in the yard. If we spread out in a field under the black sky, I picked the farthest edge of the group, and slept there.

And so the days became a long, slow trudge. Every morning we woke with the sun, and loaded up the trucks, and tied the women back up, and started walking again. Grant wouldn't tolerate questions about our destination, but we all knew there was none. We walked, and we killed, and we stole, and we ate, and then we slept and walked again.

The life after the war wasn't really an afterlife. It was a purgatory, and the living were doomed to walk in circles, while the dead gratefully sank into the dark.

～☯～

Grant sent a dozen of us into the thickets and brambles to scare up some rabbits. None of us expected to find anything. I hadn't seen a living rabbit in more years than I could count. There were a few dusty birds, their black eyes beady and mystified, and they took flight and plummeted again amid the echo of gunshots.

The men and I kept pushing deeper into the forest, and I angled away from the rest of them. More and more these days I just missed the quiet of that old apartment. I missed it more than I missed the old world, more than I missed my parents or my friends. They were all dead, and there was no bringing them back. And the apartment was probably burned-out now, squatted in by others since I'd abandoned it. Probably blood on the walls, shit on the floors. That's how most of the houses looked these days.

I couldn't go back to the apartment, but I could bring a little of that quiet to me. I felt it when I drifted to sleep in the fields, a quarter-mile from the rest of the camp. It enveloped me as we trudged up the broken, weedy blacktop of another forgotten state road, as I fell behind the group, behind even the tied-up, stumbling women.

It came to me in the forest, too, as I made my way into the dim gray hollows. I could hear the other men for a little while, crashing about in the papery dead leaves, but the farther I walked, the more muted their footfalls became. I could still hear the clan outside the forest, some shouts, the sounds of camp being set up for the night.

I walked as the forest grew dark and the shadows short. There were no sunsets left in the world, just a general draining-away of the light. I missed the moonlight, the stars. There were times I forgot that there was an entire universe above the clouds. It was as if a shroud had been pulled around the Earth. Over time, we would forget everything that we had once struggled so hard to observe and learn and prove. We would forget about Jupiter and its churning storms. We would forget about the Big Dipper, about Halley's comet. We would stumble across telescopes in old department stores and never give them a second look, never wonder about the things they once made large.

I rested against a tree and looked around at the quiet forest. The trees had somehow survived the wars, but they were dying now, a bone-white rot consuming them, turning them to rot and pulp. They smelled cold — dull, as if their greenness had been scrubbed away.

I heard the whistle before I felt the burn, and then I felt it good, and looked down, horrified to see the slim line of a quivering arrow clean through my calf. I bit back a shout and fell over, and stared wide-eyed at my leg. The arrow had gone through, but the friction of muscle and tissue had slowed it to a stop. The feather-brush of its end was dove-gray. The sharp, flat head was stained with blood and bits of flesh. My flesh.

I couldn't hold it all back, and let out a low moan. Some of our men carried bows — had they circled around and shot me? Did they think I was game?

And then I saw her.

She came from the woods like a specter, dressed in a ragged costume of torn strips of cloth, all bound together to create a distinctly inhuman shape. She terrified me. Her face was in shadow, half-blanketed by a hood. She carried a bow before her, a fresh arrow slotted against the drawstring, pointed at me.

"Wait," I whispered.

I could imagine what I looked like to her. My skin, layered with years upon years of dirt and blood. My clothing, ripped and sagging and old. My beard, peppered with debris and beginning to turn gray at the roots. I was a monstrosity, tall and lanky and strong. She saw the blade at my hip, the broken old gun that had fallen out of its holster. The spinner-thing had fallen out and tumbled away, only two bullets showing.

I felt her change, a little, when she saw the book that had fallen out of my pocket.

Then I passed out.

~◦~

I woke to the grumble of a generator.

In my past life I had never seen a generator before. Who needed one? We had electric lights, electric magic. My father had just installed a toilet that read your biometrics and knew if you were actually finished shitting before you even reached for the toilet paper. The future had arrived, and it was boring. The promises it had made to us years before — they weren't enough. When it finally delivered, we wanted bigger, faster, better.

Toilets that could shit *for* you, maybe.

The generator fascinated me. It chugged loudly in the corner of —

Where was I?

I was on my back. I felt something dense but soft beneath me, and felt at it with my hands. It had a slippery surface, and I recognized it instantly, the memory of it swimming up from the past like a ball bobbing to the surface of some murky lake. All the ships went down when the end came, when the war started, but old memories rose from the depths all the time, as we picked over burned and ruined houses and found dented, rusting old coffee makers, and remembered our mothers brewing a cup for breakfast, or cameras with broken lenses and cracked cases, churning up some forgotten moment: our fathers snapping photos at our first baseball games, cheering loudly from the sidelines — *click, wind* — *click, wind.*

But this texture, the slippery, fibrousness of it — this was a sleeping bag. I knew it intimately. My mother had signed me up for Boy Scouts as a child, despite my protestations. I'd spent several nights in the woods in a hastily-constructed tent, asleep inside a sleeve just like this bag.

I blinked and blinked and looked around and realized pretty quickly that I wasn't outdoors. There were sloping walls around me, curved and rising up to form a sort of dome above my head. I shook my head and leaned up on my elbows and squinted at the wall closest to me. It was made of thousands of sticks, from large ones down to little, tiny ones, all packed together in a hardened mud shell. Leaves and irregular bits of twig jutted out from the hardpack.

The room was not large at all — maybe only a little larger than the tent of my Boy Scout days. The floor was smooth dirt, free of debris, as if it had been swept clean. The generator sat unattended a few feet away, shuddering. A thick black cable rose up, and I followed its path to a burning lightbulb.

A lightbulb. I hadn't seen one in what felt like a thousand years. It was dim, but it was glowing, and I stared at it until it imprinted its yellow worm on my vision. I blinked and blinked some more, and as my vision settled again, I saw my paperback resting on a short, square table. There was a rickety wooden chair beside it. A leaf marked a place in the pages where no leaf had been before.

A ruffling sound. A flap opened, and on the other side I briefly saw only darkness, but I heard the sounds of the forest, almost washed out by the generator. Then the woman came in, and though I didn't mean to, I recoiled.

"Oh, shut up," the woman muttered. "I've brought you a meal."

I didn't know what to think. She produced an old metal hot plate from a cardboard box under the little table, and connected it to the generator, and put a dented metal can on top. The lid was peeled back, and after a few minutes I heard tiny bubbles and smelled a familiar old smell.

"Thank the old ones for pull-tops," she said.

It was pork and beans. The smell filled the little room. She surprised me by producing an actual bowl — chipped but otherwise in fine shape — and a metal spoon. She used the flap of her jacket to take the can off of the hot plate, then poured it into the bowl.

She held it out to me. "Eat half of it. Save the rest for me."

◦◉◦

She stared at me while I ate. I tried to stare back, but the food consumed me, and I finished off the entire bowl without thinking. She didn't complain, and then I realized that I'd eaten her share as well as my own.

"I —"

"Stow it," she said. "I'm a big girl."

It was my turn to stare now, and she held my gaze, unflinching. Her skin was scabbed and deeply tanned, with a flush of burnished red beneath her cheeks. Her lips drew thin across cracked and missing teeth. Her hair had been hacked short without regard for appearance, its ends uneven and split and dark. She was cast in stark shadow, the light of the bulb turning her hollows and slopes ominous and black.

But her eyes captivated me. They were set deep in her face, shrouded in darkness, tiredness. They were vibrant brown, almost golden, and I could see orange flecks sparkling in her irises even from a few feet away.

"Enough," she said, and looked away.

She was remarkable.

I leaned forward and grunted at the stabbing pain in my leg. "Fuck," I said, wincing. I remembered, then, and shot an accusing gaze at the woman. "You shot me."

She nodded, unmoved. "Only in the leg."

"That's enough to kill someone," I said.

"You're well enough." She jerked her thumb towards a bag beside the generator. It was torn and old, but I could see through the open zipper that it was stuffed with bottles and packages. Bandages. Salves.

I looked down at my leg for the first time, pulling the flap of the sleeping bag away. My pants had been cut away — torn away, judging by the ragged strips of cloth — and my leg was packaged tidily in brown wrapping, like something that might have arrived at your doorstep in the mail, back in the old days.

She was still staring at me when I looked back.

"You shot me," I repeated. "And — you bandaged me."

She nodded.

"Why?"

"Why did I shoot you?" she asked. "Or why did I save you?"

I thought about this. "Both."

"You're one of *them*," she spat.

I didn't answer. I knew what she meant.

She glanced at the book with the leaf in it, then back at me. "But you had that."

"It's a book," I said.

"I never saw one of them interested in books before,"

she said. She turned over a flap of her weatherbeaten coat to show me the knife underneath.

My knife.

"I took it as a sign," she went on. "That maybe you might be different. Maybe you ran away. Maybe you had enough of the killing and the raping. Maybe."

I stayed quiet.

"But I haven't stayed alive and alone this long because I'm a fool," she added. "So if I'm wrong, it won't trouble me none to open you up."

"Even after you already patched me together," I said.

She nodded slowly.

We sat like that, quiet, for a while. The generator filled the space with a throaty sound. Finally she said, "I'm going to tie you down now."

∽◎∾

She switched the generator off after strapping me to the creaky cot. The lightbulb faded to a soft cinder, then puffed out in the dark. The quiet was unnerving after the persistent rumble of the generator. It took a long time for my head to clear itself of the sound, but it did, finally, and I heard the sounds of the world swim up softly from outside.

She was silent in the dark, except for the tiny groan of the wooden chair when she shifted.

"You sleeping?" I asked after a time.

A long pause, then: "Can't."

"Why not?"

"Put yourself in my skins," she said. "Would you sleep if you had a killer in your house? Tied up or no?"

"That's what this place is?" I asked. "Your house?"

"Close enough."

"Where are we?"

"Show you in the morning," she said. "If you go the fuck to sleep."

I lay still in the pure black, then said, "Did you like the book?"

She took her time answering.

"It's good," she said, almost begrudgingly.

"I read another by her once," I said. "Long time ago now. Found it."

"I liked her version better," she replied. "Of the end."

I shifted a little, and felt her tense up in the dark.

"Easy," I said. "I'm just stretching my good leg. It's cramped."

She was still, and I imagined her gripping the knife in the dark, wondering how close I might get before she knew I was up and moving.

"Easy," I said again. "I'll keep talking as long as you want me to. So you know I'm still over here."

She didn't answer.

"What did you mean?" I asked. "When you said you liked her version better."

"The book. Her end of the world."

"Liked it better than what?"

"Than this," she said, and I heard an ache in her voice.

She woke me hours later. I couldn't remember falling asleep.

"Come on," she said.

The flap I'd seen her come through the night before was open, and cold gray daylight speared into the dark of the room. I looked around, seeing it better in the light. It looked like a beaver dam to me — the walls really were mud, clumped up and dried fast around a skeleton of twigs and rocks and pine cones and leaves. The floor was earth, brushed clean of pine needles and debris, and for the first time I saw a hollow in the center of the floor. It was full of ash and ringed with stones, and I looked up to see a tiny hole of daylight high above me.

"The hell is this place?" I asked, struggling to get up. I put my palm on the wall to steady myself, and she leaped forward, batting at my hand.

"Careful!" she fairly shouted, grabbing my wrist. "It's not that sturdy."

I looked down at her hand, then up at her dirty face.

"Sorry," I said. I put out my hands. "Help me up."

She took my left hand in her own, gripping it hard and strong. I held out my right hand.

She held out a stump.

Her eyes were unashamed and fierce.

"Jesus," I said. "How did you—"

"I don't want to talk about it," she grunted, thrusting her stump into my free hand. I gripped her forearm, and she pulled me to my feet.

The pain was sharp, like electrocution, and I almost

fell. I would have, if she hadn't grabbed me around the waist.

"We'll find you a crutch," she said.

I nodded, gasping at the fierce pain.

I hopped next to her, and she bent me over, helping me through the short doorway, and the world spilled over me in a rush. I heard the rustle of trees in the dead wind, felt the chill of morning. She came out beside me, and I saw her bright for the first time, and realized that her skin was dark-complected beneath the dirt. She saw me notice, and set her jaw, hard.

"You don't see many black girls," she said.

I shook my head. "In my —"

She stared hard. "In your what? Your tribe? Your gang?"

I swallowed. "Clan," I said. "That's what they call it, the clan."

"Appropriate," she said, and I could feel anger burning beneath her like magma.

"Grant says to kill them," I said. "He only lets the men have —"

"White girls," she finished. "Is that right?"

I nodded, hollow inside.

"Yeah. Starting over never felt so much the same," she muttered. She let go of me and I fell over, scrabbling for something to hold me up, coming up with nothing.

"Shit," I uttered, my leg alight. I rolled onto my back, and froze.

Her house rose up like a wasp's nest, an impressive, industrious achievement. It was pale and dust-colored, bleached the same rotten gray-white as the trees, and I guessed that from a distance it would vanish into the forest like a mirage. It was spackled together with mud and twigs on the inside, but on the outside, large broken branches were affixed to it.

She noticed my appreciative stare.

"Surprised?" she asked. "Ever seen a white girl build anything like that?"

"I don't think white or black has anything to do with it," I grunted, sitting up in the dead leaves. "I'm just — it's fantastic. You built it?"

"Course I built it," she said. "You think someone just left it here for me? Big 'For Rent' sign on the tree?"

"How long have you been out here?"

"Year," she said. "Maybe more. I can't tell any more."

I studied her in the pale wash of light. She wasn't pretty, but she was alive, her eyes urgent, her body tense. She had somehow survived in these woods for a year, all by herself. What's more, she did it with only one hánd.

"You got away," I said. "How did you do it?"

She regarded me calmly. "I killed a man," she said. "And then I killed three more. And I ran."

⤳❧⤸

We talked throughout the morning. She made me sit inside her nest — that's what she called it, the nest — and she sat outside with the flap open. If someone came along, she explained, I was too weak to get inside quietly and quickly. I asked if people came along often, and she shrugged.

"Every few weeks, maybe," she said. "These woods aren't deep in the mountains or anything. You saw what's just out there — fields, farms. There's an old Wal-Mart a half-mile away, if you go that-a-way. Sometimes someone cuts through the woods. Sometimes people hunt here. Ain't nobody around here permanent, though. They're always passing through."

"Like our clan," I said.

"You're the biggest group I've seen in a long time," she said. "Since I went on my own, I think."

"I thought that cutting off hands was Grant's own invention," I said, nodding at her stump.

"Guess not," she answered.

Her hand was gone below the wrist, and the stump was dull-looking, like the burl of a tree.

"Cauterized," I said.

She nodded.

"I can't imagine."

"Wasn't the worst thing I ever felt," she said. "Wasn't even the cutting-off part."

I didn't want to ask, but I did.

"It wasn't even his cock," she said, staring into the distant trees. "I expected that to be the worst, like someone taking a hot poker to me. It was bad, real bad, but the worst —"

She trailed off, and I let the quiet swallow us up. We listened to the rattle of leaves in the breeze. There was nothing else — no animal sounds, no traffic noises. The world was a boneyard, and we were ghosts.

"It was his kiss," she said, finally. "He told me not to bite him or he'd split me open like a peach. Those were his words. *Like a peach.* Then he kissed me like a man kisses his wife." Her eyes were empty. She touched her chin absently. "I didn't kiss back. He broke my jaw and knocked out my teeth. I didn't care. It meant he wouldn't kiss me again."

She turned and looked at me, her beautiful eyes haunted. I could see the slant of her jaw now, the way it didn't quite close like it should. The way it pushed out the right side of her face where it hadn't healed properly.

"Sometimes the things that are supposed to be nice hurt the worst," she said.

I thought about touching her hand.

I didn't.

~∞~

That evening she asked me about the book.

"I don't see your kind with books," she said.

"My kind."

"Killers. Marauders. Thieves." She pulled out the hot plate and cracked another tin can. More pork and beans. "Your kind."

"I —"

I wanted to protest, but I couldn't. She wasn't wrong. I was a killer. I did steal.

I sighed. "The first book I ever took was in an

apartment," I said. "I squatted there, right after — right after. Whoever lived there didn't need it any more."

"They had books."

I shook my head. "No, not books. A book. Just one."

She peered into the can, then stuck the bent spoon inside and stirred gently.

"What was it?" she asked.

"I can't remember," I answered. "It's been too long."

"But you remember that's where you first stole a book," she said.

I nodded. "Yeah. I didn't think much of it. I considered it home, or as close as I had to home. All the stuff inside was someone else's, once, but then it was mine. I didn't really steal the book. It was mine."

"So you've stolen more books."

"Yeah," I said.

"How many?"

"Just one or two, now and then. As many as I could carry without getting in the way." I sniffed the air. "Smells good."

"You don't get first bites this time," she said, and then she smiled, a crooked, half-cocked smile that warmed me, broken teeth and cracked lips and all.

"Okay," I said.

She poured the contents of the can into the bowl. There were still bits of yesterday's pork and beans stuck to the sides, but it didn't matter to her, and it wouldn't have mattered to me, either. I was certain that she'd eaten right off the ground in the last twelve months, and I sure as hell had, too. We could have reminisced about dishwashers and frozen dinners and fresh vegetables, but why rub salt in the wound?

"What did you do with them?" she asked. "The books."

"I kept them, if I could. If Grant let me," I corrected. "He didn't take kindly to my collecting things that weren't warm enough to fuck or strong enough to take a punch."

She was unfazed by my words. She spooned beans into her mouth, then passed the bowl to me.

I took a small bite, and passed it back.

"Thanks," I said.

She nodded and kept eating.

"I read them, when I could," I said. "We were always moving, so I only had time to read before nightfall, if we stopped early, or maybe before we packed off in the mornings. If we stayed in one place more than a day or two, I could find some time."

"You kept it secret," she said. "Didn't you."

"Yeah. Secret as I could, I guess."

She handed the bowl over again.

"What was your favorite book?" she asked. "Before."

I chewed thoughtfully, then said, "I didn't have one. I didn't read unless I had to."

"Sports?" she asked.

"Sometimes. Video games. TV."

"You were lazy."

"I was a teenager."

She took the bowl back and scraped the last bit of the food into two small mounds. "One for you, one for me," she said.

"You eat them both," I demurred. "Please."

She didn't protest.

"What about you?" I asked. "Did you have a favorite?"

She didn't hesitate. *"Childhood's End,"* she said. "It was my dad's favorite, and he used to read it to me, before I was old enough to know what the words meant."

"What was it about?" I asked.

"The end of humanity," she said. "Sort of. It was about losing your power."

"Prescient."

"Now there you go," she said, cracking that smile again. "I bet your overlord Grant doesn't know a word like that."

I laughed, maybe for the first time in years.

"You have a favorite now?" she asked.

I thought about it. "I read most of a book called *A Prayer for Owen Meany*," I said.

"Most of?"

"It was wet. Some of the pages had come apart, some were torn out."

"You read it anyway," she said, nodding. "That's a man hungry for knowledge."

She leaned forward onto her knees, putting the bowl aside.

I leaned forward, too, close to her raw, woodsy smell, to her eyes like amber in the bulb light.

"I got a thought about you," she said. "I got a

thought that you aren't a killer."

I looked down and away.

"No," I said. "I am."

She put her hand on my knee. "I know you've killed," she said. "But I think maybe you're not a killer."

∽◎∾

She kept me for a time. The days blurred into weeks and months, and I don't know how much time really passed. Walking wasn't getting easier for me, so she would leave me in the nest for hours, sometimes overnight, and vanish through the woods, moving soundlessly over leaves that should have crackled under her feet. She would return carrying books, and she would read to me, and we would talk about the past, and wonder at the future. Neither of us really saw much of one. She thought that humanity would multiply and regress, roving the American wastelands like packs of wolves, its population unchecked. She thought that we would evolve in a different way than before, a stupider way. She told me she could see mankind coming to a place, one day, where it didn't see the ruined buildings and houses and roads as part of its own history, but just part of the world, something accepted but never investigated.

"Our history will slip away," she said, "and one day everything will be overgrown, and we'll have forgotten things like Dr. King's speech, or NASA, or basketball. We won't remember any of it. We'll stumble across an old museum and stalk through it looking for food, not giving the old paintings a second look. They'll be no different to us from a pretty flower on a bush. Our brains will wipe themselves. We'll grow up like animals, live like animals."

She asked what I thought, but I preferred to listen to her talk about it. After those first few days together, she talked a lot. I guess it had been a long time since anybody had wondered what went on in her mind, had asked her how she felt or what she wanted.

She listened to stories of the books I'd lost along the way, the ones that I salvaged while Grant or his asshole men were throwing them off of the back of the trucks. Most weren't books that could be considered classics, but pulp stories were just as entertaining in the dark, quiet nights in the nest.

I never put myself on her, or asked her to sleep beside me on even the coldest nights. What kept us warm, what filled us with color again, were the stories, the conversations.

She listened to the horror stories. She asked me about them, and I told her — about learning to cut a man's throat, about watching the firelight the first time the hungry clan decided that the bodies could be cooked. She listened, and then she patted my hand, and as we both fell asleep in the dark, she'd whisper, "You're not a killer. You're redeemed."

"So are you," I said back.

She encouraged me to write a book about the after, about my life and what it became. About the nest, about her. She promised to find paper one one of her trips out, and she did, returning one day with a yellowed notebook. A few pages had been written on, and she wanted to tear them out, but I told her to leave them. We read them together, not understanding them at all.

Project AKBON kickoff congregational. June 11.

Attending: Michael Schwartzbaum, Digital Marketing VP; Sarah Lindeman, Marketing Manager.

The ask — A cross-channel campaign to support a confidential product launch. Codename AKBON (maybe new interactive TV consumption platform?). Launch December 4. Development co-production.

I started writing on the next page. Each night she would read my words, making corrections here and there.

"You're not a very good writer," she said, laughing. "What were you doing in high school?"

"I liked pot," I said.

But she asked for more every day, and before long the notebook was half-full. I wrote small and laboriously, my hand cramping, and every fresh sentence that I wrote conjured memories I hadn't thought of in a million years. I wrote about high school graduation, remembering at first only the gowns and the ceremony — and then an image of my mother swam up in the dark, baking a cake to celebrate, standing over the oven, her hair in damp rings on her neck, the sun pounding the house. The air conditioning unit had been broken. I remembered sleeping naked in my room, a chair propped under the doorknob so nobody would walk in, the sheets cast off of my bed, the window open, an oscillating fan washing warm breaths over me throughout the heavy night.

Every word was a spark for her. She read them slowly, sometimes returning to a line to savor the image of it — not the words, because I couldn't write *pretty*, but she liked to tell me that I took photographs that lived, that was my achievement as a writer.

We settled into a pleasant routine, one reminiscent of the old days, of couples that shared a room without talking. She would sit in her chair, reading, and I would stretch out on the cot, bent over the notebook, writing. We passed long evenings this way, forgetting that the world outside had jaws, that it was populated with men turned into wolves.

Then the lightbulb popped.

~◦~

I'll get more on my next trip out," she said. "I'll go in the morning."

"We could just start a fire," I said. "Use that little pit. I've never seen you use it."

"For good reason," she said to me. "Fires are like blood in the sea."

"Nobody would see a thing, not in here."

She shook her head. "I didn't build it right. The

smoke doesn't go out like it should. It fills up the nest. The hole up there is too small."

"I can widen it," I said.

To my surprise, she let me. We waited for the next rainfall, and then she helped me stand on the cot, and as the mud hardpack softened in the downpour, I smoothed it away from the edges of the hole, carefully picking out bits of twig and sticks that got in the way. I doubled the width of the hole, and she watched, pleased with the results.

"When it dries," she said, "we will have a fire."

We shook on it, and then slept.

∼◦∞◦∼

The end of the world — the end of ours — came before we had a chance to start the fire.

We had never talked about what we would do if this happened, if either of us was discovered. We were unprepared. We had grown soft — as soft as two people living in a wasp's nest in a dead forest can be. We were as battle-ready as a retired couple in a gated community. Our evening routines had been all wrong. Instead of reading to one another, or writing my memoirs, we should have been strengthening my leg, we should have been sharpening our knives.

She was out when they came, and for that I am thankful. For months I have shared her quiet, secret home, without ever asking her name, this woman with the crooked smile and piercing eyes, and it seems appropriate that when they set the nest aflame, she was somewhere in a nearby town, scuffling through dust and bones, hunting for a good book to read.

She would see the fire from far away, and she would think one of two things.

She might think that I had started a fire to surprise her, and I hoped that she wouldn't think that, because she would come running back, carelessly, to save me from myself.

I hoped she would think the other — that I was gone, that the worst had come to pass. I hoped she would never return to the woods, that she would find a new quiet hiding place, and tuck herself into shadow and wait for the worst to pass.

But it was never realistic to think such things. The world and its civil walls had crumbled years ago. Death comes daily to the scrappiest of survivors, and they are cast aside, glistening heaps of bones and urine and blood, as if they had never existed in the first place.

I didn't know if it was Grant and the clan, returned to hunt me down. It seemed unlikely. They would have moved on, would have forgotten me in a few days. There were deserters from the clan every few weeks, and though we usually never saw them again, it was likely they all ended up dead themselves, fallen prey to another clan's knives, or dying from the most innocent of wounds — splinters or coughs or broken ankles.

The flap of the nest was open, giving me enough light to write by, and it was, until the end, a peaceful afternoon, gray and calm and still. I didn't notice their footsteps on the dead leaves, didn't hear the murmurs of their voices. I came to myself only when the nest *whoosh*ed alive, a funeral pyre that locked me within its flickering walls. The mud around me started to drip, and the twigs caught fire, little wet flames slithering through the growing gaps in the nest walls. The walls sagged in the heat and then sloughed inward, falling upon me almost before I knew what was happening.

The sleeping bag beneath me caught the falling, burning twigs and turned into a bed of flame. I rolled onto the dirt floor, the notebook tucked beneath me, and then the walls tumbled down, and I was swallowed whole, my final thoughts of her, my nameless friend, and of our lost opportunity to test the new chimney.

And the pain. So much pain.

⟳

I did not know his name. He never told me, and I don't know if he knew it himself. He never asked mine, and I didn't tell him. Somehow that was right for us. We were blank slates, just like the world had become.

Blank slates.

Not quite blank. If you squint, you can see the marks of what was there before. You can see what was erased and what ghosts are left behind. A slate must be washed in order to be truly blank. Everything that went before has to be sacrificed so that the new beginning is pure, unmarked.

But that's a fantasy. Instead the slate is a dirty mess, with remnants of experiments, some failed, some beautiful, all of them gone. The slate is the blueprint of a ruined city, its greatest towers and darkest slums both crumbled and empty.

This is not easy for me to write. I wonder what his last words were, what he wrote in his book while I was away. I wonder if he thought of me. I wonder if he knows who did that to him.

During my worst nightmares I never thought of taking my life, of sparing myself those horrors.

Now my friend is gone.

Today I imagined so many different ways I might join him.

I saw them today. The pack. Wolves, all of them. There are not so many — they are a small pack, dirty and vile. All such groups are like this. I have seen too many of them. I have watched from the woods as they chased down a straggler, some poor soul who traveled by day through the fields. I have seen them fall upon their prey like animals.

They stayed in the meadow beside the woods for a day, long after the fire of the nest had burned itself out. I had hoped that in their sleep the fire would spread to consume the forest. It should have. But the rot in the trees, the whiteness of them, must have stayed the fire's hand. It consumed the nest until it was gone, blackening the trees around it but leaving them untouched. Even the leaves didn't spark the way they should have.

The pack left at dawn, free to continue their perverse lives while my friend's is ended.

When they disappeared from sight, I stole into the woods, and stood in the trees staring at the black ash of our home. That is how I came to think of it — as ours, although I built it, though I lived in it longer alone than with him. I stood there and did not weep. He would not have wept for me. I mourned his lost childhood more than I mourned his soul.

When I had stood there as long as I could, I went to the nest, slowly, picking my way through the leaves. They protested beneath my feet as I shuffled through them, making whatever noises they made. What did it matter, my silence? Why should I guard myself against discovery? In the end, the wolves will find us all.

He was on the ground, a charred shape, vaguely human, surrounded by charcoal branches and black earth. I knelt beside his body, still smoking gray and hot, and I told him that I am glad I did not know his name, because he was more than his name. As a man he had betrayed the name his parents bestowed upon him, whatever it might be, and with me, he had earned a new name, one that I could never give him, that he would never know.

He saved it, and while I do not know if he intended to, I know that had become his purpose. The notebook was under his scorched body, its edges brittle and burned, but its meat intact, his words preserved in gray lead. The men of his clan mocked him — they called him the Librarian, as though saving the words of the past were a foolish errand.

His final days and months were not a fool's errand.

I said a few words, and what I said is between me and the forest. It would dishonor him to write them here, in this book.

For this book is a record of his life, and of the man he was under his wolf-skin.

This is his book.

Not mine.

In his memory, I will write my own.

THE

CARETAKER

ontrary to her expectations, it wasn't the command center window that had the best views. The windows there were small and narrow, like heavy-lidded eyes, and they were recessed into the shell of the command module. They were designed for the astronauts who sat in the tall white chairs, but they didn't show much of anything, not even stars. Just slates of blackness.

Alice had been aboard the *Argus* for three weeks before she happened upon the water filtration system closet. Eve had let her know about a clog in one of the output lines, and told her where to find the system. The closet was startlingly large, almost the size of a luxurious walk-in closet in a nice house below on Earth, but filled with an orderly tangle of slim, clear tubes and winking lights and knobs and dials. But she had hardly noticed any of it, because the opposite wall — the station's hull — was missing entirely, replaced by a wide, tall triple-paned panel of smooth, clean glass.

Inside the water filtration closet, she could see Earth below her like the top of a giant balloon.

It became her favorite place on the *Argus*. She is alone, so it isn't as if someone might come looking for her and never find her, or wonder what she was doing spending all of her free time in the water filtration closet.

Alice Quayle is in her second tour as the *Argus*'s caretaker. She lives aboard the space station between projects — watering the plants and changing the light bulbs, so to speak. Her first tour had been short, just three days, and she had spent the duration terrified. She barely slept, afraid that a wiring panel might spark and set the oxygen supply on fire, afraid that a meteor might take out the communications array. Afraid that she might break something.

Her second tour is scheduled to last until August, when the biophysicist team from Apex will join the WSA crew on the *Argus*. That is two whole months away. When the live-aboard team docks on August fourth, Alice will hand over the keys, board the excursion craft with the transport pilot, then return to her usual day job at the WLA facility in Portland.

But Alice will never see Portland again.

⁓◦⁓

Alice is resting in the water filtration closet when Eve wakes up. Alice hears the familiar soft tone echo throughout the ship, and says, "Good morning, Eve. You're up early today."

But Eve has no patience for pleasantries. "There's traffic on the military band that you should listen to," she says.

Alice has never quite gotten used to Eve's voice. It's lovely and kind and unassuming, which she finds that she quite likes in a shipboard A.I. But Eve's voice emanates from the walls of the station in an otherworldly, haunting way, as if she speaks from everywhere and nowhere at once.

"The military band isn't part of my monitoring routines," Alice says. "Am I actually allowed to listen to it? Isn't it classified? Do I have clear—"

"I have authorized clearance override," Eve says.

"Can you do that?"

"In exceptional circumstances," Eve answers.

Eve does not display anger or urgency when she speaks. The WSA team and contractors who developed her spent years studying A.I.-human interactions, and discovered that an A.I. who embodied *too much* human emotion simply paralyzed astronauts. Their stress levels would climb to disastrous levels if, during an emergency, the A.I. raised its voice. Eve's pleasant detachment made it possible for the astronauts themselves to separate their emotions from difficult or dangerous tasks, and actually improved their problem-solving skills.

But when Alice hears those two words — *exception-*

al circumstances — she feels her shoulders knot and her pulse begin to thrum.

"What do you mean by that?" she asks.

Eve notices her changed attitude. "Slow your breath, Alice," she says. "Count to twelve, and then join me in the communications module."

Alice obeys, and after the twelve-count she says, "Can't you just pipe the radio in here?"

"Certainly," Eve says.

A darker tone sounds, and then the static wash of radio traffic from 1.2 million feet below swells to fill the water filtration closet.

> *— serious concerns. Who doesn't have serious concerns, sir?*
>
> *All I'm authorized to say is that we have the situation under control.*

"That's Mission Control," Alice says. "What are they talking about?"

Eve says, "The topic of conversation is unclear."

Alice turns to the window and stares down at the planet below, moving so fast yet so slowly that she can barely detect its spin.

"Extrapolate," Alice says.

But Mission Control speaks again.

> *That's not what we're hearing over here, sir. Over here it looks pretty goddamn bad.*
>
> *I assure you, gentlemen, that we have our hands firmly*

on the ball.

"Nuclear detonation," Eve suggests. "If I were to hazard a guess."

"Nuclear —" Alice stops. "The disarmament talks? How certain are you?"

"Very," Eve answers.

When is he going to raise the threat level? We've got—

The transmission from Mission Control was swallowed in a crush of static and feedback, and Eve disabled it. The water filtration closet fell into relative silence, the only sound that of the rumbling, churning equipment behind the wall panels. Alice barely notices.

She stares down at North America, where a bright flare, like a single pulse of a strobe, flickers and then vanishes.

A fat cushion of smoke billows out, then seems to rise, and Alice realizes she's staring at the expanding head of a mushroom cloud.

SIX HOURS EARLIER

Alice squeezes the silver package. The contents — *French Toast with Syrup,* the label read — have the strangest texture, but taste quite good. It's like drinking dinner through a straw, she had thought the very first time. She has a difficult time selecting her meals, entranced by the broad selection and the novelty of their state. *Salisbury Steak with Mushroom Gravy. Spinach and Feta Cheese Wrap. Chicken and Dumplings.* All of them liquefied, most prepared warm. She enjoyed the sensation of eating this way — of tasting all of the different components of the meal at the same time, as a unified flavor. There were even special holiday-themed meals. *Roast Turkey with Cranberry Sauce.*

She cheated and ate that one a few days ago, though it was June. It was better than her mother's Thanksgiving dinner.

Eve remains inactive during Alice's morning routine.

Alice had asked Eve about that during her first tour. "Why do you need to switch off?"

"I don't," Eve had explained. "But it's been shown that you and the other WSA crew function better when given regular allotments of personal space. When do you prefer yours, Alice?"

So Alice had asked for the morning to herself. She knows that Eve isn't really inactive, that she is never inactive. Eve constantly monitors the *Argus*'s many systems, and speaks up when necessary, to inform Alice of something that might need attention. But she's also a fair conversationalist, and Alice often finds herself craving another voice, even if the owner of the voice is a chipset somewhere deep in the space station's brain.

Her morning routine isn't much different from any other she can think of. She imagines that a lighthouse keeper goes through similar steps, checking the bulb's brightness, and — and what else? A lighthouse keeper probably isn't the best comparison. Perhaps a night watchman at a power plant, tapping dials and nudging switches and writing down results and such. She's amused by this, because her friends in Portland always assumed that her job might be sort of glamorous.

"I'm not much more than a house-sitter," she often explains. "I make sure the toilets aren't left running and the dishes get done."

Eve wakes early.

"Morning, Eve," Alice says.

"There's a beacon from Mission Control," Eve says.

"You don't ever say good morning, you know," Alice grumbles.

She tucks her notepad into her hip pocket, then goes to the wall and yanks hard on a thick plastic handle. A wide desk tray comes down and snaps into place, and Alice flips open the keyboard and display that are tucked into its surface. The screen glows white, then blue, and she sees the notice from Control.

"It's just a news bulletin," Alice says. "It's not even priority one."

"I assigned it greater importance," Eve says. "My counterparts at WSA recommended it."

Alice taps the screen, and the bulletin unfolds.

Priority 2. Upgrade possible. Reports from D.C. that disarmament talks have broken down.

"Okay," Alice says. She looks up and around, never certain where she should direct her comments to Eve. "Is there something that I should be doing about this?"

"It is enough that you are aware," Eve says.

NOW

Alice presses her hands against the glass. "Eve," she breathes softly. The glass fogs, then clears. Below the *Argus*, more explosions appear, even as Alice watches. She has a clear view of the States, and the explosions are happening everywhere. There are plenty in the big cities — New York is completely obscured behind rising, spreading black smoke — but she is stunned to see orange blossoms inland, in the deep midwest, along the Canadian border. There are more than she can count within moments, and before too long she realizes that she can actually see the missiles, like tiny, glowing sparks kicked up from a fire and cast into the grass.

It occurs to Alice that she should be documenting this. Somebody will want to write the chronology of events, and her unique vantage point would be invaluable to them.

"Eve," she says. "Take video beginning twenty minutes ago."

A tone chimes, and Eve says, "Retroactive video recording begun."

Alice clears her throat. "Audio, Eve."

Another tone. "Recording."

Alice is quiet for a long time. She watches the Earth below sizzle and burn, and the detonations, so small from her viewpoint, begin to spread. South America, falling into shadow as the planet turns, spits and dances with light, and Alice finds it difficult to breathe. In the east, on the farthest horizon she can see, are spiraling, twisting clouds, like enormous gray tree trunks pushing up from the ground.

"I —" she begins, and then stops. "This is Alice Quayle —"

Eve says nothing, and Alice fights hyperventilation, forcing herself to breathe slow and deep, slow and deep.

A few minutes later, she begins again.

"This is Alice Quayle, caretaker of World Space Administration station *Argus*," she says. "Eve, time and date?"

"It is eight-forty-one Pacific Standard and WSA local time," Eve says. "The date is June fourth, two thousand seventy-six."

Alice swallows, then clears her throat again.

"Beginning about twenty minutes ago," she says, "I witnessed the first of many — what appear to be nuclear attacks on the United States. I can see — oh god —"

She stops, watching as a fusillade of missiles collide with the East Coast like sparklers, and her breath catches in her throat.

"I — the — the eastern seaboard has just — has just been bombarded," she continues. "I can see the incoming missiles. I — but I can't see anything outgoing. Nothing — um — nothing is launching from the U.S."

Alice opens her mouth to try to describe what she sees on the horizon, outside of the States, but Eve interrupts.

"Alice," she says.

Alice turns away from the window and slumps against it. Her head falls back against the glass. The loose knot of hair on the back of her neck comes apart and spills onto the collar of her jumpsuit.

"Yes," Alice whispers. She feels the effect of what she has seen like burning cinders in her belly. She wants to leave the window, to go to the command module, where the windows show only darkness.

"I've received a communication from Mission Control," Eve says. "They've passed along a message from your wife."

Alice's eyes well up, and she slides down the window. "No," she rasps.

"Shall I read it to you?" Eve asks.

Tears spill down Alice's cheeks, and she presses her eyes shut tightly. She nods. "Oh, god, *Tess*," she says, her voice tight. "Read — no. Yes. Read it."

"The message is truncated," Eve says. "It reads I love. That is all."

Alice feels the wail rising in her throat like a nitrogen bubble. She opens her mouth, and it comes out and fills the empty corridors and modules of the *Argus*, and Eve is quiet as Alice slides to the floor of the water filtration system closet and sobs.

She wanted to be an astronaut.

Her fourth-grade assignment, still tucked into the pages of her memory book, was the first recorded expression of Alice's dream. What I Want to Be When I Grow Up, by Alice Jane Quayle. Her mother had treasured it, happy to see Alice dreaming of something significant. Over the years she'd collected photographs of Alice, more records of her progress: Alice in cap and gown, then in her flight suit on the deck of the U.S.S. *Archibald*, and in the cockpit, waving at the camera. A picture of Alice and Tess standing in front of the WSA museum in Oregon. Another of Alice climbing out of the training pool, weights still strapped to her arms and legs.

She was passed over year after year, despite her qualified status. Missions flew without her. The new shuttles began to go up, two or three times a month, and astronauts began to record their second, fifth, twelfth flights while Alice remained grounded. She never complained, but she was embarrassed. She thought often of the people who had given so much to help her make it so far — and how disappointed she was in herself for somehow failing them, for remaining Earthbound while her peers rocketed into the sky on columns of fire.

The caretaker offer came in her fourth year. She had wanted to turn it down, for Tess's sake, but it was Tess who convinced her to go.

"I'll always be here when you come home," Tess had said. "And the months will pass like nothing. You'll be having so much fun!"

The space station is quiet except for a faint, distant *beep, beep.*

Alice has fallen asleep on the floor of the water filtration closet. Eve disables the shipboard gravity so that Alice will sleep more comfortably. Alice's body floats off of the floor and hangs suspended before the wide window and its portrait of a world smoldering and black.

Alice wakes, and immediately begins to cry again. Her tears swim over her face like gelatin, collecting in the hollows beneath her eyes and around the ring of her nostrils.

"Gravity," she says. She rotates herself and points her feet at the floor, and drops when Eve activates the drive again. Alice's tears cascade down her face in sheets, and she pushes her palms over her skin, clearing her eyes.

She turns around and looks down at Earth. The smoke and debris has begun to crawl high into the atmosphere, as if a dirty sock is being pulled over the planet. In a few hours the ground will be blotted from view, and she shudders when she imagines the people on the ground, staring up at the sun for the last time, watching it vanish behind the sullen sky.

"They're all going to die," she whispers to Eve. "Aren't they?"

Eve says, "I observed more than three hundred distinct detonations in the United States alone. The odds of survival are infinitesimally small with only a fraction of those numbers."

JASON GURLEY · 79

Alice nods. She can see her own reflection in the glass, laid over the darkening Earth.

"Tess," she says again, too tired to cry. "My parents — I'm glad that they were dead. Before."

Eve is quiet.

Alice notices the faint *beep*ing sound. "What's that?"

Eve says, "The communications link to Mission Control has been severed. It's a standard alarm."

"Disable, please."

Eve does, and the station falls eerily silent.

Alice says, "We were going to have children next year. After we put some money aside."

Eve doesn't say anything.

"Tess wanted a boy," Alice says. "She wanted to name him after her dad. Ricardo was his name." She laughs, but it's a tragic, bitter sound. "I hated that name. I thought it was such a cliche. I wanted a girl, but I didn't know what I wanted to name her. I was going to sit with her under the stars and show her the constellations, and show her the *Argus* when it floated by, and tell her that's where Mommy worked."

A new tear slides soundlessly down Alice's cheek.

"I'd have told that to Ricardo, too," she says. "I'd have loved him even with that stupid name."

Eve says, "Perhaps you should sleep again. I can prepare a sedative."

Alice shakes her head. "Look at it," she says. "It looks like an old rotten apple, doesn't it."

Eve says, "It does look something like that."

Alice nods. "I'm glad you can fake it," she says.

"Conversation."

Eve says, "I'm glad, too."

～§～

Alice sleeps for nearly twenty hours. She barely moves, and wakes up stiff and creaky like a board. When she wakes, she gasps, and then falls back onto her pillow and presses her palms against her eyes, and cries. She dreamed of Tess, that they were in their shared bed in Portland, talking about the day. Tess had wanted to drive to Sauvie Island for fresh strawberries.

But Tess is gone, and Alice is alone.

Except for Eve, who says, "Good morning, Alice."

Alice blinks away the tears and swallows the deep cries that shift inside her like tectonic plates. *You have to stop,* she thinks. *She's dead. Everyone is dead. It can't be changed. Mourning isn't going to help now.*

Eve says, "I've prepared coffee."

"Thanks," Alice says, grunting as she pushes herself upright on the cot. Then she blinks. "You did it."

"What have I done?" Eve asks.

"You said 'good morning.'"

"You seemed distraught," Eve explains. "It seemed like it might help."

Alice nods, then shakes her head to clear the beautiful nightmare. "Right," she says, her voice a little thick. "Coffee."

～§～

Over a shiny packet labeled *Gallo Pinto* and another packet labeled *Coffee — Black*, Alice says, "So. What do we do now, Eve?"

Eve says, "There are no protocols for this."

"I can't believe that," Alice says. "Control thinks of everything."

"There are related contingencies, but nothing for an extinction-level event," Eve says. "The most obvious runner-up is a nuclear detonation that ends communication with Mission Control."

Alice puts the coffee down, the packet crumpled and empty. "Close enough," she says. "So what's the plan?"

"Maintain," Eve says, simply.

Alice looks up and around. "Maintain," she repeats. "*Maintain?*"

"Correct," Eve says.

"Just soldier on, is that right? Keep tapping the gauges, keep clearing the clogs. That's what we're supposed to do?"

"Correct."

"What's supposed to happen then?" Alice asks, her voice rising. "We maintain, and *then* what? The white horse, the rescue party?"

"In ordinary circumstances, a rescue shuttle, that's correct," Eve says. "Each location is assigned a number, and they report their status constantly. If launch site 1 is unable to stage a rescue mission, then launch site 2 fulfills the mission."

"How many launch sites are there?"

"There are twelve," Eve says.

"And how many are reporting their status?" Alice asks, pushing her half-drained packet of rice and beans aside.

"Zero," Eve says.

"So that contingency plan is out," Alice says. "Clearly."

"Correct," Eve says again.

"Which means my original question still stands, Eve. What do we do now?"

Eve says, "Maintain."

◦◦◦

Alice does not want to go back to sleep, so she stays awake for nearly two days. She orders Eve to close the windows, and thin steel shutters crank into place all over the *Argus*. She has Eve dim the lights, and shut down the power in any modules she isn't using. Eve disables gravity to save power.

"I've already done so," Eve says. "There are local aspects of the contingency plans which are still relevant. We are recycling oxygen on a six-day schedule, for example, and then we jettison forty percent and replace it with fresh stores."

"I almost don't want to ask," Alice says. "But how long can we hold out up here?"

Eve says, almost apologetically, "I will remain active indefinitely, short of any physical damage to the memory core."

Alice sighs, her dark hair floating about her face.

"How long can I hold out?"

"Longer than you may suspect," Eve says.

"Food?"

"Adequate stores for a crew of six for forty-eight months," Eve answers.

Alice stops and stares at the ceiling. "There's enough food for *twenty-four years?*"

"A single crew-person eating at the expected rate would have adequate stores for nearly one-quarter century," Eve confirms.

Alice closes her eyes. "That should make me relieved," she says. "But now I feel like I've been given a death sentence. I'll only be fifty-seven."

"Fifty-seven is not an insubstantial fraction of the expected female life span," Eve says.

"It seems insignificant when you realize that you *could* have lived to one-twenty," Alice says. She touches the hull wall lightly with her fingers and sets herself in motion, turning a slow flip. "But given the circumstances, maybe twenty-four years should feel like a prison sentence."

"You have adequate space," Eve says. "You are not incarcerated."

"I have inadequate *company*," Alice snaps. "I — oh, fuck you, you wouldn't understand."

Eve is quiet for a moment, and then a tone sounds. "Shall I put myself to sleep?" she asks.

"*Yes,*" Alice grumbles.

Eve?" Alice calls. "Come back."

The gentle tone pulses, and Eve returns. "Alice."

Alice doesn't say anything for a long moment, and then: "I feel like I should apologize. That's really stupid."

Eve says, "If I were human, I would accept. But there's no need. You have the expected responses to stress. I would express concern if you did not."

"I was really tired," she says. "I still am."

"You have not slept," Eve acknowledges. "Perhaps you should."

"Perhaps," Alice says, and closes her eyes.

She falls asleep, her knees tucked to her chest, and floats undisturbed for hours.

~ৡ৵

Alice."

Nothing.

"Alice, wake up."

Nothing.

Eve sounds a sharp alarm, a single ping, and Alice starts awake.

"*Jesus,*" she says. "What's going on?"

Eve says, "Communication."

"*What?*"

~ৡ৵

There are two distinct signals."

Gravity has been restored, and Alice stands in the communications module, staring at the wide, gently curved screen. The display is separated into three zones. On the largest of them, a flat map of the world is displayed as clear gray line art. The remaining two zones are blank.

A small circle appears on the Pacific coast of North America.

Alice's mouth opens. "Oregon?"

"In the approximate region where the city of Eugene is located," Eve confirms.

"How strong is it?"

The second zone lights up on the screen, displaying an analysis of the signal. The numbers are small, and Eve says, "Quite weak. I'm surprised that we received it at all, considering the density of the likely cloud coverage."

Alice bites her lip. "Okay, don't play it yet — tell me what I'm supposed to do with this."

Eve says, "What do you mean, Alice?"

"I — why are we listening to it?" Alice asks. "Am I even going to be — what do I do?"

"It is a distress call," Eve says. "It has broadcasted unanswered for over one week, to my knowledge. I do not detect any answering signals on Earth."

"Yes, but — it's going to be bad," Alice says. Her eyes are wide and worried. "Eve, it's going to be people crying or screaming, and I'm going to have to hear those voices in my head for the next twenty-four years.

If I can't help them, I don't think I want to listen to it."

Eve says, "I have transcribed it as well."

Unbidden, Eve displays the transcription on the screen.

Alice says, "I don't want to read it," but she does anyway.

> *S.O.S.*
> *S.O.S.*
> *Mayday? Can anybody — <distortion> — us? Hello?*
> *<distortion>*
> *<interference>*
> *— six of us. My name is Roger. My wife is here. We — <distortion> — bleeding. He needs medical attention. Hello?*
> *<interference>*
> *—water.*

"Jesus," Alice says. "There are survivors."

"Yes," Eve says. "That was always likely."

"How old did you say this message is?"

"I detected it retroactively," Eve says. "It appears to be eight days old."

"Are they still broadcasting?" Alice asks.

"The signal is repeating," Eve says. "It has looped six times per hour for the entire eight days."

"But nothing new," Alice says.

"I haven't detected any change in the broadcast, or any new signals from that region."

"They could be dead."

Eve says, "Yes. It is likely that they are dead."

"But if six people in Oregon are alive, then there could be more people there," Alice says. "There could be groups of people all over the place."

"That's also likely," Eve agrees.

"Tess," Alice says.

"Statistically unlikely," Eve says, "but possible."

Alice takes a deep breath, exhausted by having cried so much during the passing days.

"You said two signals," she says. "Is the other from the U.S., too? Are there survivors somewhere else?"

Eve says, "I cannot map the second signal."

"Why not? Interference?"

"The second signal does not originate from Earth," Eve says.

∽◉∾

Wait," Alice says.

The *Argus* takes on a gently creepy atmosphere, and Alice feels exposed, standing in the only lit compartment, with blackness chewing at the edges of her vision.

"Wait, wait," she says again. "It's radio emissions from a star. Right? It's noise."

Eve says, "It is a clear, repeating signal."

Alice focuses on her breathing. In, out. *Slower*. In... out. In... out. *Okay*. Okay.

"What?" she says.

"It is pattern-based," Eve says. "My software is analyzing the signal, attempting to decrypt the patterns."

"You can't make sense of it?" Alice asks.

"Eventually, perhaps," Eve says. "I believe that it can be decoded."

"So translate it," Alice says. "How long can it take?"

~୧୨~

A very long time, as it turns out.

Alice continues her morning routine. She inspects the oxygen levels, recharges the water tanks, replaces a bulb here and a filter there. She discovers in Eve's possession a vast record of books, the oldest of them predating the Bible, the most recent a science fiction novel published three days before the bombs.

"Ironically, an apocalypse tale," Eve says.

"No, thank you," Alice says.

She selects *The Martian Chronicles*, by Bradbury, and when Eve finishes reading the stories, Alice says, "Again," and Eve reads them aloud again. Alice listens to the story of Walter Gripp, the man who stayed behind on Mars while his fellow immigrants rushed home to Earth at the first sign of war. She doesn't much like Genevieve Selsior, the gluttonous woman who remained on Mars as well for the sole purpose of looting candy stores and beauty salons. But Walter speaks to her, and she finds herself settling into his character like a comfortable slipper.

"Call me Walter," she says to Eve, and for a few days

Eve does, and then Alice grows tired of being called Walter, and she is Alice again.

Nine months pass.

Alice shaves her head, tired of her hair drifting into her eyes and nose as it grows long. She asks Eve to hound her about exercise, and then she grows angry with Eve for nagging her. But she exercises. Despite the activity, she feels herself growing slight, and her bones feel spindly.

"Food stores might not be the limiting factor," she says to Eve one day, and Eve gives Alice a physical and administers supplements and weekly CS4 shots to keep her fit and strong.

She begins to spend some time each day in front of a camera, recording her memories. She speaks to the camera shyly at first, then more confidently as time passes. She tells the story of the the roof she climbed when she was nine, and how it sagged and collapsed beneath her, and she broke her arm. She talks about her parents, and the time they renewed their vows, and a thunderstorm soaked everyone in attendance. She tries and fails to remember something from every year of her life, but discovers that the years and stories have blended together, and she no longer remembers clearly how old she was when something happened to her, or which of their many houses her family lived in at the time.

Eve reads *The Time Traveler's Wife* to her. Alice doesn't like it. It reminds her of Tess too much. Eve recommends Kipling, but Alice grows bored after a few pages. They read Dickens and Joyce and Maugham. Alice's favorite is *Cakes and Ale*. Eve reads Margaret Atwood and Michael Crichton, and a biography of Abraham Lincoln. Alice falls in love with Joan Didion and Oliver Sacks, and so Eve reads memoirs to her for a time, until Alice grows tired of listening to the stories of real people who are most certainly dead and wasting away, if not already turned to dust and ash, on the withering planet far below.

Eve suggests a movie, and Alice agrees, brightening at the idea, but as soon as she sees the visage of another human being, walking and talking and running and kissing and eating, she bursts into tears and demands that Eve turn it off. From then on, Alice does not ask for more books, or music, or movies. Everything that Eve says reminds Alice that she is possibly the last surviving human, or at least soon will be; that she exists in relative comfort here in her floating aquarium two hundred miles above a boneyard.

⤜◈⤏

E ve is silent for weeks, for Alice has grown more and more fragile.

The end date of Alice's tour passes, and Eve does not acknowledge it, concerned that the milestone might unravel Alice's poor psyche further. The day goes by, and no ship docks in the slip, and no airlocks hiss open and shut, and no crew of English and Russian and Chinese scientists and astronauts and cosmonauts comes aboard to shake Alice's hand and send her home again.

The date passes in absolute silence. Alice does not say a word, and lies in bed all day without sleeping.

⌇⌇

Alice," Eve says.

Alice jumps.

She has grown accustomed to the quiet. It has been fourteen weeks since Eve last spoke to her. She may have even forgotten that Eve was there.

"What do you want?" Alice says.

"I have translated the message," Eve says.

⌇⌇

Alice is herself again instantly.

She stands at the display. All three zones of the interface are blank this time. Eve is not able to display a map large enough to pinpoint the origin point of the signal. Alice remembers the last time she stood here, and says, "Eve, is the Oregon signal still broadcasting?"

Eve says, "It ceased about two months ago. But there are other signals now."

Alice says, "Others?"

"The cloud coverage is thinner," Eve explains. "You haven't seen it, because the windows are shut. I have received nine new signals in the last week."

"Nine?" Alice asks. "People are still alive!"

"Seven of them are also looping signals," Eve cautions. "They could easily have been broadcasting for an equally long time, and may not be true messages any longer."

"The other two?"

"One originates in Italy, and the remaining signal comes from Louisiana," Eve says. "They are talking to each other."

Alice stares at the blank screen. "I — can I hear?"

Eve says, "You wish to hear the audio?"

"Yes, yes," Alice says. "Play it."

An audio spectrum appears on the screen as Eve engages the message.

Half of the conversation is in Italian, and sounds like a very old man. The other half belongs to a woman in Louisiana with a scratchy, powerful accent. The woman does not speak Italian, but Alice can hear the relief and joy in her voice to even be speaking to another living soul.

"What is the Italian man saying?" Alice asks. "Can you translate?"

Eve says, "'My grandchild was born yesterday. I do not think he will survive, but his birth is a miracle nonetheless. His mother did not live through the birth. My daughter, my daughter. I cannot raise this boy alone. I have no food for myself. I have already eaten my poor sweet Claudio. I miss his company when I sleep. I do not know if I can bear to watch my grandson die. I have a sweater. He will not feel a thing. I will find a way to follow him. The grief will take me into the dark after him.'"

Alice is aghast.

The Louisiana woman does not understand anything that the old man is saying. The two people seem to be communicating simply by listening to each other, and telling stories. The woman hears the man out, and then she tells the man about her grandfather's plantation house, and visiting him there as a girl, and she begins to weep as she talks about her husband's death, the heat that sizzled the paint right off of her car and tumbled her off of the freeway and into a ditch, wheels up, half-buried in muck — she did not think she could have survived if not for the accident.

She begins to talk about the black creeping poison she can see working its way up her leg, her foot long swelled up too much to walk on, the toenails splitting and oozing.

"Enough," Alice says.

Eve ends the audio. "There is the other transmission," she reminds Alice.

Alice's eyes are red and tired. "Okay," she says.

∽◉∾

It has been crudely translated into English," Eve says. "The original message was a series of mathematical expressions and patterns, a near-universal language."

"I don't care," Alice says wearily. "What does it say?"

Eve says, "I have simplified the message as much as possible. I believe I have preserved its intent."

"Read it," Alice says again. She slumps into a desk chair with a heavy sigh.

"The message reads: 'Greetings and peace. In the vastness of space, all life is family. Good fortune to you. May we meet in peace someday.'"

Alice looks up at the screen, dumbfounded. "Holy shit," she says. "You're fucking with me. You have to be."

"It is a crude but sound translation," Eve says. "I have error-checked my work many times over to be certain."

Alice blinks rapidly, then opens and shuts her mouth. "Holy shit," she says again.

༺⚭༻

Time seems to slow down.

Alice stays in the chair, shaking her head.

Eve says, "There are no other messages. What would you like to do?"

Alice looks up at the blank screen, then turns in a slow circle in the chair. "Do?"

"The message seems rather historical," Eve says. "Perhaps it should be commemorated."

"Do you mean —"

"You could send a reply," Eve suggests.

Alice says, "It would take years to arrive! Wouldn't it?"

"The message is quite old," Eve says. "The origin point is very far away. It would likely have taken over two hundred years to reach us."

"Exquisite timing," Alice complains. "Can you imagine? They just missed us."

"They did not miss you," Eve points out.

Alice shuffles her feet and drags the chair to a stop. "That message would get there long after we're all dead."

"But it would confirm their hopes," Eve says.

Alice smiles a tired smile. "You're an optimist."

"I'm programmed as such," Eve says. "I have astronauts to care for. You're — delicate."

Alice laughs. "I think that's the most human thing you've ever said."

⚬⚬⚬

Alice sleeps that night, and dreams of a root cellar. The walls are sod, reinforced with heavy planks of old, rotting wood. The roots of deepset trees have pushed between the planks, into the seams, and have crawled into the socket of empty space so deep beneath the earth. A generator rattles in the corner. A bare bulb dangles over a metal shelf stacked with swelled cans of food, the labels dried and sagging off. There are bugs everywhere — cockroaches scuttling over the pantry shelf, spiders staking out the high corners and the gaps in the invading roots.

"Hungry," a voice whispers, choked and thin, and

Alice turns to see a shape in a rocking chair.

She looks at the shelves, and sees an open can of syrupy peaches. Alice sniffs them. They smell sweet, a little cloying, but unspoiled.

"Peaches?" she asks.

The rocking chair person nods, and the chair creaks.

Alice finds a bent spoon on a lower shelf, and picks it up, shaking a beetle off of the handle first. She carries the spoon and the peaches to the chair, and kneels down.

"Here," she says, scooping up a spongy slice of saturated peach. "Eat."

She feeds the shadowy person. The first few bites go down, but then something plops into the dirt. Alice looks down and sees a chewed hunk of orange peach lying there, spotted with grime and bits of blood and dirt. She looks up at the person in the chair, who shrugs, still in shadow, and croaks, "Sorry."

Alice looks down and sees a gaping, chewed-apart hole in the person's gut, and as she stares in horror, the second hunk of peach slides out of a rotten pucker and tumbles into the dirt, too.

"I loved you," whispers the shadowy person. "I wish I'd been up there with you instead of not."

Alice recoils, and wakes up, and says, *"Eve!"*

∽◎◡

*— six of us. My name is Roger. My wife is here. We —
<distortion> — bleeding.*

Alice says, "They're all dying. You could hear it, too, couldn't you?"

I have a sweater. He will not feel a thing.

Eve says, "It is not an inappropriate conclusion."

"I wanted to save them when I heard them," Alice says. "But I can't do that, can I."

"You are not equipped to save anybody," Eve says. "If you returned to Earth, you would not survive the fallout. You don't have adequate supplies or protection."

"Right," Alice says.

My toes are breaking up. I think it's gangrene. But it might be radiation. Hell of a thing, ain't it?

"I'm the last woman," Alice says. "They're all going to die."

"There may be survivors yet," Eve says. "There are many shelters and safe zones, even in such terrible scenarios."

"But it won't ever be the same. They'll have to stay underground for fifty years, they won't be able to farm or hunt. It will be a miracle if they survive, or ever come out."

Eve does not disagree.

"Play it again," Alice says.

"Which message?"

"The important one. Don't read it. I want to hear it."

≈

I t sounds like enormous metal gears, turning and cranking and lumbering. Now and then there is a grating sound, as though a piece of metal has fallen in between the teeth and is being gnawed and shredded.

"It is not something that ears alone can parse," Eve apologizes.

"It's —" Alice pauses. "Sort of beautiful."

Eve is quiet.

"Will you read it to me again? The words?"

Eve says, "Of course."

> *Greetings and peace.*
> *In the vastness of space, all life is family.*
> *Good fortune to you.*
> *May we meet in peace someday.*

Eve falls silent.

"It's like the most beautiful poem ever written," Alice says.

She and Eve are quiet for a time, and then Alice says, "I can't imagine why you would let me do this," and she tells Eve her plan.

Eve listens, and says, "Do you wish me to calculate the probability of success?"

"No," Alice says.

"Very well," Eve says. "I will help you."

Alice sits in the cockpit of the excursion ship.

"Twenty-four years was a prison sentence," she says.

Eve says, "It was not even likely you would live so long."

Alice scoffs. "You told me I had adequate stores for twenty-four years!"

"Humans are fragile," Eve says. "There are emotional factors that I cannot compute accurately. You likely would have succumbed to a human condition that I cannot project with any certainty."

"What condition are you talking about?"

"Loneliness," Eve says.

"Eve," Alice says, pulling the heavy restraining straps over her shoulders and jamming the buckle home. "Everybody on Earth is dead."

"Not yet," Eve interrupts.

"Dead," Alice repeats. "Or close to it."

"Yes."

"Everyone is dead or almost dead, and I'm healthy and well-fed and going crazy on a metal dirigible a million miles above a dead world."

"Two hundred thirty-four miles," Eve corrects.

"Two hundred thirty-four miles," Alice says. "And we've just received confirmation that we aren't alone. I might be the last woman, but I'm not the last living thing *anywhere*."

"There are other life forms alive on Earth," Eve says.

"You're a buzzkill," Alice says. "This is my *one giant leap for mankind* moment. Are you recording it?"

"I record everything," Eve says. "Although on this vessel my storage capacity will exhaust itself in a shorter amount of time."

"How much time?"

"Sixty years, approximately."

Alice considers this.

The excursion craft is small and neat. A photograph of the transport pilot's family is displayed on a small, square screen on the control panel.

Greetings and peace.

"Are you certain you do not with me to calculate the probability of your survival?" Eve asks again.

"You've already done it, haven't you," Alice says.

"I have."

"Fine. What are my odds?"

Eve says, "One in—"

"Wait, wait, no, no, don't — I don't want to know," Alice says loudly. "I don't want to know. Okay?"

Eve says, "Very well."

In the vastness of space, all life is family.

"The extra oxygen stores will help," Alice says to herself. "Extra food. Medical supplies. Eve, did you bring books?"

"I did not know you had an interest any longer," Eve

says.

"Shit. Eve, did you? It's going to be a long trip."

"I have four thousand volumes," Eve says.

Alice smiles. "Okay. I'm nervous, can you tell?"

"Your heart rate is higher than usual, but still within reasonable limits."

Good fortune to you.

"The odds are pretty long, aren't they?" Alice asks.

She detaches the excursion craft from the *Argus*, and it descends gently. She watches the docking collar recede.

"It depends on how you define 'pretty,'" Eve answers.

Alice accelerates, and the craft darts into the spreading black. The *Argus* falls quickly into the small craft's wake.

"We should name her," Alice says. "This little ship."

Eve says, "Might I suggest a name?"

"Shoot."

"Perhaps you might christen it the *Santa Maria,*" Eve says. "There is some historical significance."

Alice thinks about this. "No," she says, finally. "Let's call it *Tess.*"

May we meet in peace someday.

The *Tess* carries Alice and Eve deep into the darkness.

Eve says, "You have considerably less than twenty-four years now."

Alice says, "Maybe they'll meet us halfway. Do you think?"

THE
WINTER
LANDS

He has had the coat for many years. It is long and made of wool and is the color of rust, with a faint herringbone pattern and smooth wooden buttons. It doesn't quite match his winter cap, but he doesn't mind. The earflaps keep his sagging ears warm, and the sheepskin lining hides his thinning hair and pale, spotted scalp. He wears ancient gloves, the leather softened by time, and grips a gnarled wooden cane in one trembling hand.

He moves slowly, drawing stares as he makes his way down the street. The crowds bustle around him in cargo shorts and flip-flops and T-shirts. He pays them no mind. He is not interested in their darkening suntans, their glistening skin, the beads of perspiration on their necks. He doesn't notice that people watch him.

The warm spell of the last few weeks has not broken. The old man plods on, oblivious to the heat. Sweat trickles down his brow and collects in his unruly white eyebrows. It seeps into the deep creases of his tired face, as if sweat has carved those grooves over the decades. His breath comes in slow shudders. His body is curved like a comma, his shoulders high and round, his head tucked low. He can barely lift his eyes to see more than a few steps ahead.

It takes him nearly two hours to hobble to the bookstore. A streetcar runs along the avenue between the shop and the old man's home, a small studio apartment in a retirement community, but he has never trusted public transportation more than his own two feet, no matter how much they ache. He barely notices the pain anymore.

The bookstore is older than he is, a stack of bricks that will soon be empty. It has been marked for destruction in just a few weeks. A notice, posted by the city, identifies the building as structurally unsound — an unreinforced masonry building that may be unsafe during earthquakes. The old man hasn't felt an earthquake in these parts in — well, in his entire life. The building predates the war, was in fact heavily damaged by shelling, and clumsily repaired. Over the years its walls have begun to lean, just like the old man himself.

To bid farewell to the bookshop's grand legacy, its current owner — the great-grandson of the shop's founder — has scheduled a week-long parade of author readings. Celebrated writers from all over the world have come to the old man's little borough to read from classic novels, or their own new releases. In the gaps between these high-profile appearances on the schedule, the owner has scheduled open-mic readings, inviting the public to come and enjoy the opportunity to read their unpublished works in the historic shop before it disappears forever.

The old man clutches his cane in one hand and a sheaf of pages in the other. The papers are yellowed and old, grown thin with age. They crackle, tied into a bundle with twine. He has brought only a few pages — a dozen, no more — and has not given any thought to whether his voice will permit him to read even that much. He has nobody to talk to anymore, and has never made a habit of talking to himself, so his voice is sometimes quiet for weeks on end.

At the shop, a slim young woman spies him struggling with the door and rushes to help him.

"Oh, let me assist you," she says.

"Thank you," he says, and his voice is not so haggard. It sounds like rocks in a tumbler, but it is clear enough, and even a little sonorous.

She notices the papers in his hand. "Are you here for the readings?"

He nods. He cannot see her face — it pains him to lift his neck so high, and he feels a bit like an old lech, for this puts his eyes level with her breasts. She does not seem to notice, however, and he follows her pointed finger toward the back of the shop.

It has been hollowed out for the event, the shelves pushed to the wall to make room for fifty or sixty aluminum folding chairs. A velvet rope separates the gallery from the rest of the shop, and a felt signboard reports that the Heisel reading has just ended, and that the open readings will commence at four o'clock.

He pauses beside the sign and pushes the cuff of his coat away from his wrist. The bulky watch beneath reads 3:44.

The young woman appears at his side again. He does so wish he could see her face.

"May I help you to a seat?" she asks him.

He allows her the kindness, and she seats him in the front row — near the aisle, he suspects, so that he will be easy to attend to if he should suddenly die. Sudden expiration is a necessary consideration these days, and he takes care to always wear clean shorts, just in case.

She holds his elbow as he lowers himself into the chair with a long sigh, then crouches delicately at his knees.

"Can I bring you some water?" she asks him.

He knows what he must look like to her. He can feel the thin line of sweat over his ribs, the dampness of the loose skin beneath his jaw and chin, behind his ears. His eyebrows are wet, and some of the sweat has sponged out of the wiry white hair onto the bridge of his glasses. A single drop slides down the glass, and he almost crosses his eyes focusing on it.

"Water," he says, "would be very kind."

She goes and returns a moment later with a paper cup, and pats his hand.

"Can I take your coat?" she asks him. "It's very

warm out."

"But cool in here," he says. "No, thank you. I'll keep it."

"If you need a thing —" she begins.

He nods. "Thank you."

He settles into the chair, shifting this way and that until he is reasonably comfortable, and waits. He puts the water cup, untouched, on the seat beside him, then tucks his chin to his chest and closes his eyes.

∽◉∾

His name is Jonathan Froestt.

In the fall of 1958, after sending away hundreds of copies of a short story in a plain yellow envelope, and receiving hundreds of polite — and a few quite rude — rejection letters, he sold his first and only short story to a pulp magazine called *Fantastic Wonderful Tales*. The story was entitled "The Forgotten Winter Lands." The magazine's editor, a patient old fellow by the name of Abraham Gendry, had accepted the story "despite its rudimentary properties," as he wrote.

"Your tale is both fantastic and wonderful," Gendry had written, "though your writing, sadly, is neither. It's nothing a little editing won't fix."

Gendry had enclosed a check for ten dollars, which Froestt never cashed. The story was published in the magazine's September issue. It had been heavily edited by Gendry himself.

The story was about a military sniper named John

Frost. ("Clever disguise," Gendry wrote.) In the tale, Frost is sent into the dusky hills high above a German village with his spotter, a soldier named Jankel. Frost and Jankel find a cliff dense with foliage. There's a clear line of sight to the village church, a narrow building with a tall bell tower that overlooks a plaza. Frost burrows into the bushes, and Jankel climbs a tree to serve as lookout.

They've been assigned to take down a German general. For days they watch the church. Intelligence suggests that the general and his men are holed up deep inside the structure, perhaps in a subbasement. Frost doesn't know what the general has done, and he doesn't ask.

Days pass, and nobody emerges from the church. Frost and Jankel take shifts on the cliff's edge, sip water from their canteens, and munch ration bars, and otherwise speak very little. On the fourth day, Jankel's shift at the scope ends.

"I don't think they're here," he grumbles to Frost, who scoots into place with the rifle.

"You know our orders," Frost says. "We wait."

And so they wait. But they are tired, and Jankel falls asleep in the tree. Frost concentrates on the church, employing his sniper's training to slow his heart rate, his breathing, to dim the world around him. He does not hear Jankel's light snores. He doesn't feel the rain that has begun to fall. He doesn't feel the tiny hunger pangs in his belly. For him, there is only the church, and nothing else in the entire world.

When Jankel awakes, Frost lies still in the bushes. Hours pass before Jankel realizes that Frost hasn't stirred, even a little, for some time. He hisses at Frost, who doesn't answer. He climbs out of the tree and crawls to Frost's position, and grabs his partner by the ankle.

Frost's boot is freezing cold, to Jankel's surprise. He grips both of Frost's feet and yanks him, inch by inch, out of the bushes. Jankel discovers, to his horror, that Frost is frozen solid. The rifle is locked in his blue fingers.

In the story, this is an unusual development because it is not winter. The story takes place in the peak of summer, when it is hot enough in the German countryside that both soldiers sweat while sitting still in the shade.

In Froestt's original draft of "The Forgotten Winter Lands," Jankel abandons Frost on the hillside and returns to base. Gendry, whose brother had served in the war, found this unrealistic, and modified the story. In the published story, Jankel drags Frost back to base, dodging German patrols and moving by night. It takes two days — two days of hauling a heavy, icy corpse across sweltering hills — but Jankel succeeds. Frost is declared dead by a field doctor — who in both drafts seems rather unsurprised to find that Frost has become an icicle — and his body is parked on a gurney in the morgue tent while it waits for extraction with other casualties.

But Frost thaws out, and when he does, he reanimates, startling a nurse and raving about a beautiful white snowbound world where men can be gods. "You have to let me go back!" he yells at the medical staff. "They need me there!"

He is quarantined and interviewed by several army doctors, and tells each the same story in almost identical words: he quieted his body, as any good sniper does, and eventually fell into a sort of fugue. The world blurred out around him, and then so did the world he saw through the scope. He felt calm and relaxed, and then, in his mind's eye, he saw a red door. It opened, and he went through it, and when he emerged on the other side, he was in a white world of ice and snow and sun. He called it the land of winter, the doctors reported, and described sparkling ice castles that were no taller than his belly. These structures were inhabited by very small, very human-like beings that Frost called the Snowlings.

"Patient reports that these Snowling creatures received him as a god, and petitioned him for help," one doctor reported. "Patient is clearly delusional, and I recommend a medical discharge for psychiatric reasons."

In the story, Frost is indeed discharged. He returns to America, where his family is disillusioned by his strange rants about the winter lands. Frost's wife takes the children and leaves him. He is unable to hold a job, and eventually, as he grows old, his eldest child returns and puts him in a retirement home with medical supervision. To his death, Frost talks of almost nothing except for winter and the Snowlings. He hammers at a typewriter, producing page after page of complete drivel — rambling passages about quests and kingships and storms and gods and ice. He is found dead in his room one morning, his lips blue, skin pale and drained of color. His body radiates cold.

The story ends rather abruptly. Frost dies, and when he opens his eyes again, he stands in the winter land, surrounded by the Snowlings, revered and welcomed into their tiny arms. The story is a curiosity at best, readers seemed to think, and only a few letters to Gendry mentioned it. None celebrated it; one reader described it as "neither fantastic nor wonderful, but interesting."

It was the only story of Froestt's that Gendry would publish, though he received a plain yellow envelope in the mail, once per week, for the rest of his life. When Gendry died in 1974, the envelopes were marked "Addressee Deceased" and returned to Froestt, who never submitted another story to any publication ever again.

∽◎∾

The old man wakes up with a start. He looks to his right. His water cup is gone, replaced with a human being. All of the chairs around him are occupied now, and he struggles to sit up, aware that he has slumped a little toward his neighbor during his unexpected nap.

"I'm sorry," he whispers loudly into the person's shoulder.

The room feels almost full, and the old man suddenly feels very out of place. He doesn't belong here, really. He is not an accomplished writer, only a persistent one. The small apartment he occupies in the retirement community is mostly unfurnished, except for a twin bed and a lonely chair and end table. The rest of the room is stacked with cartons. They are ancient and so stuffed with paper that their squared-off sides bulge, their flat bottoms sag. At some point over the years he ran out of cartons, and could no longer find the model that he preferred, so he simply began stacking loose paper on top of the boxes. Towers of typing paper clutter the apartment. He has filled the cabinets in his kitchenette with pages. The icebox contains reams of them. His dish rack has never seen a dish, but holds several hundred loose sheets of paper that fold and curl over each other.

He has written of the winter lands for more than sixty years. His writing has not improved with practice. It employs a passive voice, and is richly populated with fragments of sentences, and he has never learned the difference between an adjective and an adverb. He frequently shifts from a first-person perspective to a third, and sometimes misspells his hero's name, using Frost and Froestt interchangeably.

A woman writer stands at the dais now, reading from a short story that is, so far as Froestt can tell, about a bastard who gets his in the end. She reads nervously, but with a certain shaky confidence, and at her last line — "He sits up, looks around, and never sees the car that lops his head off like a cantaloupe" — there is a polite smattering of applause.

Froestt can only see the woman's legs as she walks away, and the legs of the man who steps up to the dais next. His pants are well pressed, his shoes shiny brown leather. His voice is reedy and he says, "We've got a few minutes before Heidi Johannsson arrives, time for one last reader. Any volunteers?"

Several hands go up — the old man can hear the rustle of sleeves and pages — and he lifts his cane into the air and waves it around.

The man at the dais hesitates, and then the old man sees a familiar pair of legs approach the dais — the girl who brought him water and helped him to his seat. He lowers his cane, certain that she will intervene for him, and she does.

"The gentleman with the cane," the fellow at the dais says, and then the woman appears at Froestt's side to help him up. She walks with him to the dais. His feet squelch in his shoes, his socks damp with sweat. She notices, and with kindness asks if he will be all right. He nods and whispers a rattly thanks.

Froestt is small and hunched at the dais, and cannot crane his neck enough to see the man who has welcomed him there.

"What's your name, sir?" the man asks.

"Jonathan," Froestt says.

"Jonathan," the man repeats. "And your story? What will you be reading to us today?"

He tips the microphone down. Froestt clears his throat and says, "I'll be reading from my novel."

"What's your novel called?"

"The Forgotten Winter Lands," he says.

"Catchy title," the man says. "I assume you've been sending it to publishers?"

Froestt can feel the crowd's alternating curiosity and disinterest in his story. Sweat dribbles down his nose. He shakes his head and says, "No publishers. It's not finished yet."

"Well, I wish I could say that I hope we'll see it on our shelves one day," the man says. "But I wish you luck in your writing, and let's all give Jonathan a round of applause for joining us today."

The soft patter of hands fades quickly. The woman from before steps up and helps to adjust the microphone to Froestt's height. She covers it with her hand and says, "You're sure you're okay? I can't take your coat? You seem awfully warm."

"Thank you," Froestt says again. The microphone squeals a tiny bit.

He cannot see the audience, but he can feel their stares. The thin trickle of sweat down his ribs is now a steady stream. It soaks into his clothing, and then his coat.

Someone whispers, "The poor man is going to have heatstroke in that coat."

The coat quickly soaks through and turns almost black with moisture.

"The Forgotten Winter Lands," Froestt reads, his voice like a crumbling wall. "Chapter One."

A puddle collects at his feet. Moisture drips from

his nose, from the soaking flaps of his hat. His glasses fog with condensation, so he removes them, and holds his pages closer to his face. The paper becomes soggy in his hands, and the ink of his words begins to run, but it is no matter, for he knows the words by heart after all these years.

He puts the paper down on the dais. By now the audience is chattering audibly about the poor man and his condition. Someone says, loudly, "Give the man some water," and another person says, "That's unnatural. Someone should call an ambulance." Froestt hears the words *overheated* and *pass out*, but he ignores them, and narrates his story aloud.

"John Frost was a sniper of the highest order," he says. "He is known for taking all of his shots and not missing one. Never even the hardest of them."

Someone groans softly.

"His friend is Martin Jankel, and they have been friends since the beginning," Froestt continues, closing his eyes. He feels his breathing even out, and the words soothe him. His heart, pounding so hard moments before, calms to a patient *thump-thump*, and each pattern of beats further from the beats before. "Jankel is the spotter in their sniper team, and Frost is the sniper, and they are both quite good. Together and apart, but mostly together."

Froestt's clothing grows saturated with water. It drips from his sleeves, from his dangling hands, from his chin and nose and brow. The puddle around his feet spreads. It leaps and dances with each falling drop from above.

"I have to ask you to stop," says the host, who steps delicately through the widening pool of water and puts a hand over the microphone. "Sir, are you — what is going on? Are you all right?"

"You look terrible," says the girl. "Come, sit down while we call an ambulance."

Froestt shakes his head. "I'm quite all right," he says. "Call an ambulance if you must, but please, let me read until they arrive."

"Sir," the man protests.

Froestt leans back as far as he can, until he can just glimpse the man's eyes.

"Please," Froestt says. "I've truly waited a lifetime for this."

The man looks at the girl, then back at Froestt. Then he raises both of his hands, palms out, as if to say *All right, it's not my problem — I tried*. He backs away, then says, loudly, "Let's continue."

Froestt nods and turns back to the microphone.

"On the day that it all happened, Frost and Jankel were sent to the hills beyond an enemy post," he reads. "Their task was to assassinate a very evil general. He was the most evil general there was, at least at that moment of the war. This was World War Two."

Another groan from the audience.

Froestt's eyes close as he imagines the words. Sixty years of words — millions of them, stacked carefully in his apartment, unread, unpublished. He is old, he is tired, and he supposes he intends to read here until his novel is finished. He will ad-lib the ending if he must, but the ending cannot be told until — until he knows what it is.

The ambulance arrives at the front of the shop, its turning lights washing the gallery and the shelves in blue and red. Two uniformed men enter, carrying a collapsed stretcher between them.

Froestt doesn't look up, but the host approaches him again. "Okay, sir," he says. "They've arrived. Why don't you come with me —"

"My ending," Froestt says. "Is this it?"

The man says, "Yes, sir, it's time for you to go."

He puts his hand on the dais and reaches for Froestt's arm. Froestt recoils, just a bit, and leans on his cane heavily. The twisted wood makes a cracking sound that reverberates through the shop, and someone gasps, and then the cane shatters like ice. Brown and black shards explode outward like little frozen chips, and Froestt's eyes widen, and he stumbles backward, away from the host.

"Whoa, there —" the host says, and in that moment four people dash towards the dais: the host, the woman who had brought Froestt his water, and the two emergency personnel who have only just arrived, and who drop their stretcher as they run for the old man.

The girl is somehow quicker than them all, and gets one hand behind Froestt as he tumbles, and she feels his heavy wet wool coat go slack as he falls, and then she hears someone scream, and Froestt crumbles into a shining wet pile of clothing and snow, and the gallery falls utterly silent.

⁓᷄⁓

The rest of the program is rescheduled for the following day, and the host dismisses all of the guests from the store, and locks the doors. He returns to the dais, which has been moved aside, and watches as the ambulance technicians shuffle around, unsure what to do.

"Lucy," the host says to the girl, who still rests on her knees beside the melting heap of bluish snow.

She looks up at him. "He was real," she says, dazed. "I touched him."

"I think you should let these men talk to you," he says, nodding at the medical team.

"He was real," she repeats.

The men take her out of the store to the ambulance to check her over. When they've left, the host walks over to the damp pile of snow and old clothes and kicks at them with his toe. The old man is gone, as if he had never been there. The snow fades quickly under the shop lights, turning to water and running away in rivulets across the wood floor.

"Huh," he says.

There's little else to say.

He bends over and grabs the collar of the old man's coat and picks it up, shaking out clumps of snow. The collar has a label, and on the label the words *J. Froestt* are written in black marker. The words are smeary and damp, the ink bleeding deep into the label's threads.

The host folds the coat at the shoulders and lays it over the dais, then sighs and goes to the back of the store and into a closet, and comes back holding a mop, and gets to work.

NEBULAE

BLUE PLANET

Like a great beast emerging from a black sea, the blue planet rises over the moon's horizon.

It reminds him of Earth which was.

If he could have chosen a perfect destination, he might have chosen Triton, with this view.

He could even tolerate the *Nebulae*.

For a view like this, a man could live with almost anything.

Neptune's hazy blue form was nothing like Earth, and yet, if Ansel squinted and looked just past it, his mind would trick him. It worked every time, at least until his eyes grew curious, and turned to stare at the planet directly.

Neptune was no Earth. Neptune was more

beautiful.

Gone, the structure of land masses. Gone, the ice caps. Forgotten, the towering mountains. Absent, the thin white wakes of boats on the great blue seas.

Instead, a vaporous orb, periwinkle blue, its skies the texture of crushed chalk.

If you listened, you could almost hear it churning, like the dull, distant roar of a waterfall.

But it was silent, as space tends to be.

❧

Up early, you.

At the sound of this gruff voice, not altogether unexpected, Ansel turns from the viewing deck.

And you as well, he says.

Grant rubs his big, dark eyes. Slept like hell last night, he says. Kept dreaming of a she-demon. She had teeth for eyes, and — well, she had teeth everywhere. Slept like hell, you know.

Sorry to hear it, Ansel says.

Grant waves a hand in dismissal, and starts working on a pot of coffee.

Always can tell I'm gonna find you here, he says. Right here, at that glass. Like the blue has a hold on you.

I like it here.

Rest of the crew thinks you've got a fixation, you know. I had a great-great-great-great-great-great grandfather, all kinds of years ago, lived on Earth, worked the fishing boats in Newfoundland. Liked to say that the sea got its gray claws into a man, wouldn't let go. Liked to say it marked a man when it met him. That it would take him one day. It's like that with you and the planet.

Ansel shrugs. I don't mind.

They want to know why you're here, actually. Grant pours a cup of coffee and sits at the long mess table. I'd like to know myself, if you want the truth. You're not our newest addition, you know, but you're the most shut-up-tight one.

Ansel says, That coffee is shit.

Ah, I know, Grant says. But you do with what you've got, you know.

Yes, Ansel says. Yes, I know.

Want one?

Ansel turns from the glass. Yeah, alright.

Crystals?

Black, Ansel says.

Man after my great-great-great-great — ah, whatever the fuck. Man after my grandpa's own heart.

Tell me something, Ansel says, sitting down. How do you know what your ten-times-removed grandpa was saying about the ocean back on the homeworld?

Grant smiles. I'm a bullshitter, or couldn't you tell.

You might say I had a feeling.

I got a feeling about you, too, Mr. Agusti. I got myself a feeling you're up to something. Would that be a right thing to say?

Ansel peers at Grant over his cup of coffee. Captain Karkinnen, he says, that would be a right thing to say about every human being you know.

Grant furrows his brow, then nods in agreement. A right thing to say.

These days, Ansel says.

These days, Grant concurs. These god-be-fucking days.

~☙~

The *Nebulae*, like most satellite stations, was never quite finished. The crew quarters are full of exposed wiring and thermal plating and chunks of insulation. The restroom facilities do not have doors, but since the crew is one hundred percent male, few grumblings arise. The mess hall and bridge are the only segments of the station that resemble a finished product, and they are quite nice, with smooth-as-satin floors and transparent hull walls and faint, glowing illumination that seems almost sourceless.

Ansel has had occasion to bunk on many such stations during his seven-year tour, and the Nebulae is no better or worse than the rest.

Perhaps better in one way.

Ansel's quarters are private. He knows that the other men distrust him for this. Captain Karkinnen is the only other crewman with his own quarters. The rest of the men bunk together, six to a room, four rooms in all. It's a large crew for such a small station, and that there are no women is of no surprise to Ansel. This far out in the system, far from the eyes of the Council, women turn into victims, and then into corpses, and then vanish.

Ansel is aboard the *Nebulae* on behalf of one such woman.

One very, very important woman.

ENGINEERS

In the morning, Ansel wakes to the clatter of footsteps in the corridor. He lifts the mask from his eyes, and adjusts to the dim light. His compartment is very small, and he stretches out his arm to find the wall beside his bunk. He dresses in the dark, and carefully fits his prosthetic hand into its socket. He can feel the tiny motors in each finger whirr as the hand boots up.

There are voices outside now. Ansel goes to the door and listens.

Is that all of them?

Captain Karkinnen's voice.

Sir, we're missing two men.

Ansel doesn't recognize this voice, but this is no surprise. The men all sound the same to him. Admittedly, this is a problem. He is, after all, searching for one man among this thicket of engineers and machinists.

Which two? Karkinnen asks.

The second man sounds almost embarrassed. Well, sir — it's —

Out with it, the captain says.

It's Hawthorne and Lacey, sir.

Fuck. Of course it is. They'll be in the second engine compartment, then. Go retrieve them. Tell them to get their naked asses outside.

Sir, I — I don't want to interrupt —

Cover your goddamn eyes, then, Karkinnen says. Then tell them to get their asses outside.

Yes, sir.

Ansel listens to the captain storm away, and the sounds in the hallway disappear.

He leans on the door so that it won't squeak, and slides it open. The corridor is indeed empty, and then it isn't.

An engineer in a T-shirt comes dashing by, then stops when he sees Ansel's open door.

Hey, Ansel says. What's your name?

Jonah, the engineer says.

Joba, what's going on?

It's Jonah.

Sorry. Jonah. Ansel flicks his eyes in the direction of the airlocks. What's going on out there?

Well, you probably slept through it, Jonah says with obvious distaste. But we got hit.

Hit. By what?

By whatever the hell's floating around out there, Jonah says. I gotta go, so —

Has this happened before? Getting hit?

Happens maybe once or twice a year, Jonah says. I —

Asteroid, you think?

Well, it probably wasn't a bird, Jonah says.

Snarky, Ansel says. Good for you.

Jonah sets his jaw and walks off, shaking his head.

The hallway is empty again.

Ansel steps out of his room and slides the door shut. He walks silently around the corner, into the bunk wing. The four rooms are spaced evenly apart, two on each side of the hall. None of them have doors.

Ansel peeks inside each room.

Empty, all of them.

Time to get to work.

∽◉∾

The view is ruined, cluttered with feet and arms and tools.

Sorry about that, Grant says. You heard what happened by now, I take it.

Ansel nods. Rumor is we were shot by space pirates.

Grant chuckles and shakes his big red beard. Just the usual asteroid patter, nothing more.

Anything serious?

Some pits and dings, a few panels cracked, some knocked loose. Maybe a bit more. The boys are still crawling the hull.

Ansel tilts his head and looks out at the side of the

ship. The engineers are bundled up in their exterior suits, boxy glass helmets, tools clinging to their arms and chests for easy access.

Do they all go out? he asks.

They do, Grant says.

Huh, Ansel says.

You're thinking that's pretty stupid, Grant says. It's alright. I get it.

No, not at all.

A better captain might hold a couple men back, just in case something terrible happens.

It's space, Ansel says. Only terrible things ever happen.

They'll be fine, though. They'll fix her up, and come back in from the cold just fine.

A sudden banging sound echoes through the ship. Ansel doesn't flinch.

Found a loose one, I reckon, Grant says. Want some coffee?

No, Ansel says. How long are they outside?

Been out a couple hours, Grant answers. Be out probably six more. Then they'll sleep, eat, and go out again.

So the ship's empty right now.

Empty except for us two buzzards.

Ansel nods thoughtfully.

What's on your mind, Mr. Agusti? the captain asks.

Ansel rests his hands on the table. Seems like a good time to talk.

Talk, Grant repeats. What's there to talk about?

Let's talk about why I'm here.

Grant leans back in his chair and folds his arms. That's an interesting topic, considering I don't have any expertise in it.

I do, though.

Alright. Why are you here?

Ansel gets up and walks around the table. He takes a seat beside Grant Karkinnen, and leans in close.

I want to talk about Evelyn Jans, he says.

⌒◎⌒

The men eat dinner like wild animals, then drag themselves out of the mess hall and to their bunks. Captain Karkinnen had been wrong. They hadn't spent just six more hours on the hull. Seventeen hours they'd been outside. The sounds of their ragged snores crawl through the ship.

At four a.m., Ansel sits in the dark of his room, an old screenview on his lap. He's wearing a skullcap with a wire attached to it. He plugs the wire into the tablet, and waits.

Eventually a picture jerks into view. It's fragmented, and it freezes often, but he can make out the craggy, bespectacled face of Mirs Korski. The timestamp in the corner reads 0432 : FEB 22 2586.

Outside, Ansel hears footsteps pass his door.

On the screen, a transcription of Korski's words appear.

It's been some time, the transcription reads. Your reports have been tiresome and repetitive.

Ansel thinks, *It's true, and for that I apologize. But I have news.*

A transcription of Ansel's own words appear:
BLUE FORD HAT LOGIC FLIES HACK NEWS.

Shit, Ansel says.

He traces the wire to the skullcap's input. The jack is loose. He presses it into the side of the cap firmly.

Your last message is unclear, Korski's transcription reads.

Ansel thinks, *I'm sorry. There was a Sense malfunction. I have to transmit in secret. Is this more clear?*

Ansel's words appear correctly on the screen this time.

A long moment passes, and then Korski says, Better. Report.

I have news to report.

Each message takes six seconds to travel between the *Nebulae* and Citadel Meili, the enormous space station orbiting Earth.

Don't make me ask what it is, Korski says. I have things to do right now.

Ansel thinks, *Evelyn was on the* Nebulae, *a satellite-class station.*

Was?

She was here a long time ago.

Six seconds.

Where did she go?

She never left. That's my news.

Six seconds.

Stop toying with me. What happened to her?

It's a bit of a story.

Six seconds.

Let's hear it.

I thought you had things to do.

Six seconds.

They can wait.

SEVEN YEARS

I was captain for all of six weeks when she arrived, Grant says. Captain before me — Seamus Belwether, he was called — up and died at mess one morning. We had a doctor on the station back then, who said Belly's brain popped.

Aneurysm? Ansel asks.

Sure, and a big one, too. Old man just got this blank look on his face, then pitched sideways out of his chair. Hit the corner of the table on the way over, so there was a bit of blood to confuse everyone about what had happened.

Were you the first officer?

Naw, Grant says. Maybe just the most levelheaded on a ship of tightly-wound fools. Belly didn't do much captaining, to be fair. He had rank from the first System War, that's why he took command here. I'm not sure he ever wanted it.

He was in the war, Ansel says.

He was, for all three weeks of it, Grant says. Belly had one good leg and one that wasn't. Not too different from your hand, there, except where you've got a hand, Belly just had a metal stick.

You noticed, Ansel says.

I've got an eye for things. And a good ear. I heard the little motors first time you shook my hand. How'd you lose yours?

Ansel flexes his left hand. I was in the war, too. Working the munitions dock on one of the freighters. Wasn't anything exciting. One of the weapons crates broke free of the line, trapped my hand against a wall. Flattened it like a slice of bread.

Sorry piece of luck, Grant says. I hear the new prosthetics have brains. Yours isn't one of those, is it?

No, mine's just little gears and cogs, Ansel lies.

Funny thing, you'd think, for the captain of a satellite station to be wary of tech, right? But I am, Grant says. I've seen it do some bad things. Turns friends into enemies. Unravels the best of plans.

Grant slugs his coffee and gets to his feet. You're sure you don't want any, he says.

I'm sure.

Alright, well, if you change your mind, you know where it's at, the captain says, and laughs.

You said something before, Ansel says. You called the war the first System War.

Caught that, did you.

You know something I don't? Ansel asks.

I wouldn't say that, Grant says. But you're a fool if you think one was enough.

You think another one is coming, then.

I think several more are coming, most likely. Council isn't looked upon so kindly, you know that. Especially not by people as far out as we are. Once you get past Mars, you feel the law a little less... tangibly. Easier to go your own way when you see a Council representative once every fifty years instead of once or twice a month.

Ansel nods. You know, I think I'll have some coffee after all.

Suit yourself.

He finds a cup and pours. You were talking about becoming captain, he says.

Right, Grant says.

You said Belwether wasn't really interested in running the ship.

Not really. He was getting up there. Would've been happiest, I think, if he could've put a hammock right there in front of that window, stare all day at the blue, same as you do.

Were you different? Ansel asks.

You mean, did I want the job?

Sure.

I never really thought about it. This isn't a military vessel. It's a satellite station. We're here to work the moon. We send teams down, we scoop up some shit, we put it in boxes and we send it to the center, and a few months later we get paid. There's no real command to be had here. Someone just has to decide what to do if things go wrong.

Ansel sips his coffee. So who decided that would be you?

We took a vote, Grant says. Seemed like the democratic thing to do.

Democratic, Ansel repeats.

Haven't heard that word in awhile, I'd wager, Grant says.

No, not much.

Where are you from, Mr. Agusti?

You ask like a man who already has an idea.

Yes, Grant says. I had to hazard a guess, I'd say you're from the center.

You're not far off.

Not Mars, and not Earth. I've got a funny feeling you're Meili stock.

Ansel says, What gives you that idea?

Gut, I guess. You keep to yourself, you don't spread no ideas around. And you're asking about Evelyn, so I'm going to come right out and say it. I think you're Meili proper, sent to find her. Sound about right?

Ansel shrugs. You know where she is?

Grant finishes his coffee. I know where she's not.

And where's that?

The captain pushes back from the table, cup in hand.

She's not here.

❧

The men crawl on the hull like spiders, hammering panels back into place, ripping out the punctured ones. The sound is insidious, as if they are trying to chew their way into the ship.

You get used to it, the captain says. More coffee?

I won't finish the one I've got, Ansel says.

Shit, isn't it.

Yeah, Ansel says.

You get used to that, too. The captain takes his seat again. Tell me, though. You plan on being around long enough to get used to it?

That's up to you, Ansel says. Tell me where she is.

Grant nods thoughtfully. Well, Mr. Agusti, she's in one of two places.

And where might those be?

She's either down there —

The captain points out the window at Triton's horizon.

— or she's out there.

He points at the inky black space beyond.

Ansel says, So she's dead.

Oh, yes, Grant says. She's most certainly dead.

Tell me how.

❧

You remember what I said about the law, and how short its reach feels out here? Grant asks. You just said it, Ansel says. So — yes.

How many ships have you been on this deep in the black? *Nebulae* can't be the only one.

Nine, Ansel says.

And of those nine, were the crews uniformly male?

Yeah, Ansel says. They were.

You ever wonder why?

I've heard stories, Ansel says. Tell me yours.

Women this far out, they aren't women any more, Grant says. They're things. I don't condone it — don't get me wrong. I've got two daughters of my own, and they're safely on Luna. But this is what happens out here.

So she was raped, and then someone covered it up, Ansel says.

That about covers it, Grant says. I wish I had a more interesting story for you, but I don't.

Tell me how it happened.

You want names?

I do, Ansel says. I want the name of every man who touched her, and the name of every man who didn't do anything to stop it.

So basically the crew list, Grant says.

If they all were involved, then yes.

Who are the names for?

Tell me how it happened first.

Grant frowns. I didn't see it happen. But I was there when she was jettisoned.

She was raped?

Yes.

By one man?

By all of them, probably. You know how men are this far out in the d—

One time? Multiple times?

Grant shakes his head. Maybe you've never been on a ship where it happened before. But they — she was a kept woman, Mr. Agusti. In fact, your quarters? That's where she was kept. And she had visitors all day, all night, over and over. There are usually twenty or more men on this ship. The line doesn't ever die down.

And you knew about this.

I won't lie to you, Grant says.

Good. Don't.

I knew.

And did you —

Never.

Not once?

I would never treat a woman that way.

But you allowed others to.

Grant pushes his coffee aside. Who exactly are you working for, Mr. Agusti?

I wouldn't ask a question if you didn't really want the answer.

I'm asking.

You really don't want the answer, Ansel says.

Council? It's the Council. You're an operative.

Ansel leans forward in his chair. Captain, he says. Do you know who Evelyn Jans was?

Grant says, Just the usual, I figured. Woman who wants to do the same work the men do. Doesn't take into consideration the risks. Wants to be a miner, wants to be an engineer, wants to see the black.

Evelyn was all of those things, Ansel says.

I could tell. She was —

But she was also heir to Council seat four.

Grant's eyes widen.

You didn't know, then.

Grant stutters. I — I didn't —

I believe you. You agree we have a problem now.

I don't — I want — this is — it was seven years ago. There hasn't been a woman on-board since. Nobody's done anything wrong since —

Captain Karkinnen, Ansel says gently. Your men violated and then murdered Council royalty. It really doesn't matter if you knew who she was or not. The Council sent me to find out what happened to her, and now I have. Do you know what will happen now?

I don't know, says the captain.

What happens now is I'm going to file my report, Ansel says. And I'm going to wait for further instruction.

Ansel stands up. He slides his coffee cup down the table towards the captain.

And Captain, he says. I promise you, the Council's reach is more than long enough.

∽⦿∾

Korski says, So she is dead.

Yes, sir. I believe that she is.

Six seconds.

And you saw no body?

She was pitched out of an airlock nearly seven years ago. Her body is somewhere on the dead moon below, unless it escaped orbit. Then she could be anywhere.

The seconds pass by, and Ansel waits for Korski's response.

Ansel doesn't trust the man. Korski was born to fugitives, and when his parents were hunted down, he was adopted by an operative named Josef Korski. Mirs was only six years old when his parents were killed. Josef taught him the truth: that if Mirs's parents had been loyal to their Council, they would not have died. Over the years, his memories of his parents faded, and his loyalty to Josef and the Grand Council grew.

The boy had been raised to become an assassin like his father.

Mirs is nearly ninety now, and the Onyx laws run in his blood. He commands the largest contingent of operatives in Citadel history. There are fifteen hundred of them, each slipping silently into the black, disguising themselves as rebels, and puncturing uprisings from within. Under his command, the operatives have put down nearly one thousand micro-rebellions, most before they have even gestated.

They have killed thousands.

Ansel has no hesitation about this. He has killed dozens of people himself.

He just doesn't trust Korski to come to his aid when he needs it.

And the footsteps that pass his door in the night make him think this time he's going to need it.

~⊛~

Have you confirmed her death with ship's records? Korski asks.

I have an airlock release log from that year, Ansel thinks. *But this is a rudimentary station. There are no visual recordings. There are no personnel logs. She is not even on record as having been here.*

Six seconds.

But you believe she was, and that she was killed. Why?

I have a confession from the station's captain, sir. It's not direct evidence, but I believe the man.

Six seconds.

You will stake your honor on this? Evelyn Jans is dead?

I genuinely believe she is.

Six seconds.

If she is dead, steps will be taken. But if you are wrong, and she is alive, people will die without justification.

Sir, out here, everybody is a rebel. If they are not guilty of one crime, they are on the verge of far greater ones.

Six seconds.

Six seconds.

Twenty seconds.

Korski's image jerks and freezes, and his final message appears:

Bring honor to the Council.

EVELYN

For the hundredth time, Ansel calls up his mission summary on the old screenview. A large photograph, the most recent image of Evelyn, appears on the tablet. Beside it is a projection of her appearance now.

She's pale, with red hair cut short. Ansel would not describe her as traditionally beautiful. Her features are slightly masculine, her stare hard and confident. He idly traces his finger on the screen, rotating her image. Evelyn has narrow, strong shoulders. A long neck, not graceful, but severe.

When she left Meili, Evelyn Jans was nineteen years old. She would be twenty-nine now, nearly thirty. The projection can be skewed to reflect the effects of a gentle existence or a punishing one. Ansel switches between the two, watching Evelyn's face morph from almost genteel to rigid, her expression shift from a half-smile to a thin grimace.

He knew her, though only by association. At the annual operative's ball, when the Council would greet and celebrate the dark arts of Ansel and his fellow assassins, he had seen Evelyn dancing. She was out of place in her red gown, he had thought, with her hair up in curls beneath a veil. She seemed like anything but a Council heir. He'd watched her bypass the champagne and sneak a pull of whiskey with the servers, and he'd liked her immensely for that.

When she disappeared, he volunteered, as did a hundred other operatives.

Korski had selected him from the group.

For your particular dedication to violence as a means to an end, Korski had said. Miss Jans is of great importance to her father. Finding her would bring you great recognition and reward, and would give me increased leverage to expand our ranks. You'll have the resources you need. You will not have a home, however, if you fail.

Neither Korski nor Ansel himself had expected the search to take this long.

∽◉◠

It had taken Ansel a year just to find Evelyn's trail.

In 2580, he tracked her to Skyresh, the great city on Phobos, Mars's largest moon.

Ansel had only visited Skyresh once before, many years earlier, when it was only a surface colony, just a scattered next of domed huts and generators twisting life support cables. He had been impressed to see how much the outpost had grown, and how rapidly. It had consumed the moon, rooting deep into its core, carving out great bowls of surface rock. The city was a glowing hub by then, with spires and towers, an air rail system, a tiny spaceport, and a satellite defense system.

It was the latter feature that had led to the Citadel claiming the moon outright as a strategic asset during the System War. The war had lasted only three weeks, but even now, over twenty-five years later, Phobos is a Citadel outpost.

Ansel had been greeted by a Citadel representative named Oren Lukasic, a man with the oblong, hunched body of a pillbug.

Lukasic had been happy to see him. We don't get operatives here often, he had said.

That you know of, Ansel replied.

Lukasic laughed. A fine point. And a reassuring one.

Ansel followed Lukasic deep into the Citadel Embassy, a fine white structure that glowed like ivory in the dim sunlight.

You've never gotten the tour, Lukasic noted.

I was here once, back in the outpost days, Ansel had said. But there's no time for a tour now, Representative.

Fair to say, Lukasic said. I have not been informed of your mission, but Mr. Korski asked me to provide you whatever you need. We take personal requests from the Citadel Operative Director quite seriously. Whatever you need, you'll have.

Appreciated, Ansel had said.

They had taken an old-fashioned elevator then, and Ansel had looked up to see the polished white structure recede, replaced by sanded rock.

We're going into the moon.

We are, Lukasic said. The embassy's surface structure is a distraction. In fact, all of our strategic facilities are based in the interior.

Wise, Ansel said. But Phobos isn't a big moon. Wouldn't a strike large enough to destroy the surface structure still — well — crack this moon wide open?

This moon is far more solid than you might think. We've burrowed into it so completely that little of the original rock is left. Most of what you see on the surface is what remains. The interior is reinforced with a strut architecture. You'll see it in a moment, actually.

And he had. The elevator had emerged from the rock tunnel into a narrow cavern, visible only for a moment, that was a warren of great pillars. Worker pods flitted about, and as Ansel's eyes had adjusted, he had seen men in engineer suits crawling all over the pillars, tool platforms floating beside them.

Impressive, he had said.

The elevator dropped back into a rock chute, then slowed to a stop.

Lukasic stepped out first. This way, he said.

⚬

You know why I'm here, then, Ansel said.

Lukasic had gestured at a seat. I know a little, yes.

Evelyn Jans. She's missing.

Lukasic's expression changed. I knew you were searching for someone. I did not know it was a Council heir.

First heir to seat four. You know that Councilman Jans is the oldest ranking member. His term will expire in a decade. It's very important that Evelyn is safely returned to the Citadel so she can continue to study for her eventual role.

Of course, Lukasic had said. And you're sure she was here?

I don't know if she is here, or if she's moved on. Why do you say was?

I just assumed —

I won't remind you about operative guidelines, Representative. I'm sure you know them well.

Lukasic nodded. Yes.

Please, Ansel said, relaxing in his chair. Tell me what you know. Let's start with why you've already lied to me.

❧

From Skyresh, Evelyn's trail had meandered, almost as if she was trying to lose a tail. In a sense, Ansel thought, maybe she had been. He had wrung a confession out of Representative Lukasic

— Evelyn had not only landed first on Skyresh, but had left with a woman. A lover, Lukasic had theorized, but he hadn't known her name.

Ansel had discovered the woman's identity, but not until Io. By then, he had tracked Evelyn from Skyresh to Olympus, the Citadel's capital city on Mars. Evelyn had lingered there for six months, then disappeared again. It took Ansel nearly two years to pick up her trail again.

She'd turned up on *Ceres-11*, a mining station tethered to the asteroid belt's dwarf planet of the same name. He couldn't figure it out at first. *Ceres-11* was a roughneck station, with several thousand miners aboard. There were no amenities. Miners worked seven-year shifts, then broke for three years, then returned. In those seven years, they made enough money to support their distant families for a decade. Three years usually wasn't enough time for them to return home, then make it back to *Ceres-11* in time for the next shift, so there was extremely high turnover. Most miners didn't return.

The ones that did needed something to do to kill the time. They were making incredible amounts of money, with nothing to spend it on. The hard work, twelve hours every day, created conditions ripe for dissension. *Ceres-11* was believed to be the origin point of a revolutionary movement that had led to the System War in 2570.

Ansel started to put it together. Evelyn wasn't pleasure-cruising. Her trek through the system was loopy, but she was gradually moving outward, farther from the Citadel and its greatest ring of influence.

Evelyn was looking for a rebellion.

～◎～

It was only a theory, but he had confirmed it when he tracked her to *Promantha*, a fringe colony that orbited the Galilean moon Io. Ansel traveled there, but he didn't have to. *Promantha* was the birthplace of the Ivory movement. The Citadel monitored the colony closely, but quietly. There were rumors that there were at least seven operatives on *Promantha*.

Ansel wouldn't know them when he saw them. Deep-cover operatives identity-shifted before they went to work. Their fingerprints, their voice frequencies, their facial structure, even the color of their eyes were altered.

But he knew that they would know him.

～◎～

Promantha was the second colony in Io's orbit. The remnants of the first, *Epimetheus*, still circled the moon, a debris-field reminder of man's lack of foresight. Io's volcanoes are tempestuous and powerful, with plumes that dramatically arced into orbit. *Epimetheus* had been a victim of such a plume, and had been ripped to pieces. Two thousand people died.

There are still desiccated bodies in the debris field, forty years after the tragedy.

Ansel had hitched a ride on a medical freighter that was bound for Jupiter, where it would live forever, serving the orbital colonies that revolved around the planet and its moons. The freighter dispatched smaller ships to each of the colonies to establish contact and determine the state of its inhabitants. Ansel rode along with the crew traveling to *Promantha*.

The colony was a marvel of homegrown engineering, a collection of salvaged hulls and smaller stations that had been fused into one great, lumbering organism. It wasn't lovely to look upon, but it was intelligently stitched together.

Once aboard, Ansel settled into a comfortable routine. Temporary residents were required to work for their board, and Ansel joined the arboretum crew. He trimmed and mulched and planted, and in the evenings, he ate quietly and alone in the cafeteria. Four weeks passed as he integrated himself into the crew, establishing his face, his name, his reserved manner.

He attended meetings that were strangely anonymous and vague. Nobody said the word *revolution*. Nobody said *rebellion*. Nobody talked about the Council or the Citadel at all.

He made no friends.

He was eating dinner when the operative found him.

She sat across from him. Ansel didn't look up, but he knew who she was.

Hello, she had said.

Ansel had just nodded.

I'm from Titan, she said.

There were a dozen pass phrases that an operative learned, one for almost any sort of environment or social encounter. *I'm from Titan* was one of them. No names, no details. Just the pass phrase.

Took your time, he said.

I had to, she answered. You can't rush these things. I'm probably more at risk here than you are.

Fair enough, he said.

What are you here for? Are you deep?

Not deep, he said. This is my true face.

We have plenty of people aboard already. Are you an addition, or —

I'm here for something else, he had said. I'm looking for someone.

Who?

Evelyn Jans.

Jans.

Councilman Jans's first heir.

She tilted her head. And you think she's here?

I've got reason to believe she is, or was. She came with someone. A woman.

Who?

I don't have a name. I have a face, though. Ansel

handed his screenview to the woman. He tapped the glass. You know her?

The operative nodded her head. Yes. I know her well.

Ansel said, She might be important. Who is she?

Did you lose your hand in the war? the operative asked.

Ansel nodded, and continued to eat. The woman, he said.

Do you remember the spaceport sabotage?

Olympus, he said. It was the closest the rebellion got to the inner circle. Yes.

The woman in this photograph is Hatsuye Hayami, the operative had said. She was the rebellion's answer to a deep-cover operative. The spaceport was her.

Demolitions specialist?

Hatsuye could blow up a moon with a cup of coffee, the woman said. Specialist would be an understatement.

Is she here?

She was. You missed her by a few months, though. And if she was traveling with someone else, I certainly never saw her. I could ask around.

Do that, Ansel had said.

One thing you should probably know about Hatsuye, though.

What's that?

Rumor is she's wired.

Wired how?

The woman said, She has several prosthetics.

They're not quite as sophisticated as yours, but they're better than average. Right hand, entire left arm. One of her legs. I forget which. She's practically half-machine at this point. They say her prosthetics are wired, that she's always got her finger on the trigger.

She's a walking bomb.

Essentially.

Lovely.

TERMINAL

Seven years, always months behind her.

And now she was dead.

He wonders if Hatsuye Hayami met a similar fate. And if so, why hadn't she blown up the entire station?

Ansel sighs and takes off the skullcap. He winds the cord up, and sets it aside with the screenview.

Bring honor to the council.

Kill them, in other words.

Kill them all.

He hasn't killed anyone in years. Since before starting this mission, in fact.

He wonders if he'll remember how.

ᘎᗒᗕ

It's nearly six a.m. when he drifts to sleep.

The footsteps wake him up.

Unlike the ones earlier, these footsteps don't fade away.

These slow, and stop.

Ansel can see a disturbance in the thin reed of light below his compartment door.

He rolls over in bed and searches the bedside shelf in the dark. He finds an earpiece and puts it in.

Test, he says.

Quietly, in his ear, he hears a neutral-gender voice respond.

Test successful.

There are more shadows in the hallway now.

More soft steps.

Ansel prepares himself.

~⚭~

The door holds when they kick it in, so they kick it more, and harder. It's metal, but flimsy, and there's enough flex for someone to cram a steel bar into the gap. Someone leans into it, and the bar turns, and then the door pops open with a metallic ring.

Ansel doesn't say a word as the men rush into his room.

Nobody hits the lights.

The engineers are backlit by the hallway. They're surprisingly quiet as they grab Ansel and yank him from the bed. The crowd separates as two of the men take him by the arms and drag him roughly down the corridor.

The silence makes it weird.

Ansel is used to this sort of thing, but usually the attackers talk shit, or yell.

This is weird.

He expects a beating, but that isn't what happens.

The men pull him down hallway after hallway until they come to an airlock.

Captain Karkinnen is waiting.

We'll see how long that reach is now, the captain says.

Ansel says, I probably can't talk you out of this one, can I. Not going to happen.

The captain shakes his head.

You're not just a mining station, are you.

The captain shakes his head again.

You're rebellion, Ansel says.

Karkinnen smiles, and one of the men laughs.

You're a long way from home, Council bitch, says an engineer.

Ansel doesn't take his eye off of the captain. That's why you killed her, isn't it. You knew who she was all along.

But the captain doesn't say a word.

You killed her because she was Council royalty. Did you still rape her first?

Shut the fuck up, says another man.

I've already filed my report, Ansel says. The *Nebulae*

is on the Council's radar right now.

The captain shrugs. That's alright. Every dog has his day.

Ansel looks around. Nearly every engineer on the ship seems to be here.

Test, he says.

What? says the engineer. Ansel recognizes him as Jonah.

Test successful.

What now? Ansel asks. You're going to throw me out, just like you did her? Does that make you feel good?

We thought about keeping you, the captain says. Start a line for you, just like we did for her.

You're not attracted to me, Ansel says. Shame.

The captain's smile turns malicious. He steps back and says, Suit him up.

～◎～

Captain Karkinnen taps the faceplate.

You hear me? he asks.

Inside the space suit, Ansel nods.

We had a spare suit lying around, Grant says. Used to be hers, actually. Don't need it anymore. Thought it might be nice to let you think about things while you're out there. Try to imagine what she thought, out there alive for all of two seconds. Imagine that fear. Then hang onto it awhile. Choke on it awhile.

Ansel smiles. Pretty interesting plan, he says.

We like it, says Jonah.

The captain scratches his red beard. We're gonna leave you to it now. You can hang onto something if you want, but I hear the depressurization packs a wallop. Might pull your arms right off. You don't want a hole in your suit.

No, I guess I wouldn't, Ansel says.

He's curiously unafraid. Every operative prepares for this moment from their first day of training. Ansel never really thought that it would come, but now that it's here, he's calm.

You've got four hours of oxygen on your back, Grant says. That ought to be plenty of time to make your peace.

Peace with whom?

Oh, you know. God, or whatever you believe in.

What do you believe in, Captain?

The captain leans in close. His breath fogs up the faceplate.

I believe we're done, he says.

~❀~

Ansel stands alone in the center of the airlock. Pressed against the inner windows are the faces of the engineers. They're wild faces, wearing the expressions of animals.

So this is the rebellion, Ansel thinks. A pack of angry dogs.

Then someone pushes the button, and the outer

doors open.

～◎～

The force causes him to black out for a moment.
When Ansel wakes up, he panics.

Not because he's in the black now, just one
more body caught in orbit.

Because he might be too far away from the ship.
It hovers above him like a soaring scarab, receding
quickly. Lights wink on and off around the airlock door
as it closes. The crew has moved to the viewport in
the mess hall, gathered around the captain, a small red
figure standing in Ansel's favorite spot.

Ansel takes a deep breath.

Detonate, he says.

For the longest moment of his life, nothing
happens.

～◎～

The *Nebulae* was a familiar station to Ansel
when he had boarded. Satellite-class, mining
specialty. The station looked like a large beetle,
with wide, insectile arms that sprouted from its sides.

Onyx operatives were well-versed in common ship
models.

Learn your environments well, Mirs Korski had
taught his men. You will spend the rest of your life
in the black, on freighters, on private ships, on space

stations, on colony stations. When you board, know your exits. Know the weaknesses. Know the blind corners and dead alleys. Never be caught unawares.

Always be prepared.

Ansel's specialty was demolitions, too.

When he boarded a ship this far from Council space, at his first opportunity, he installed voice-activated charges.

A ship like this had all sorts of fragmentation points.

Ansel had chosen the one in the bunk rooms.

It was easy when the ship was empty.

⤳⟶

C ome on, come on, he thinks.

He opens his mouth to give the command again, certain he's too far out of range.

And with a tiny burst of light, the ship comes apart.

The men in the window are thrown to the floor.

One figure remains, and Ansel imagines that it is the captain.

He watches as the ship unfolds like origami.

Hatsuye Hayami could not have done a better job, he thinks.

All it ever takes is a small charge.

You just light the fuse, and sometimes the rest takes care of itself.

The ship pulls apart like a puzzle.

Ansel watches as the men spill into the black. Just like Evelyn.

～⟋⟍～

Hours pass.

The ship is in torn and scattered pieces high above him. There are sparks. Lights flicker and go dark. Fires start and are snuffed out by the vacuum of space. He has drifted far enough now that he cannot pick the shapes of the men out of the wreckage.

Everything looks so small now. He's tired of looking at the ruins.

He tries to roll himself over without starting a spin he can't stop.

A slow turn, some counter-motion, and then he's looking down at Triton. It's a pitted, cold rock. It looks like an unsplit melon.

If you've seen one moon, you've seen them all.

But beyond it, the great blue planet rises. Its surface is an oil painting, deeply saturated, rich with swirling cloud rivers and bottomless gaseous canyons. He imagines trailing his fingers in it like a man in a sailboat. What a nice sensation that must have been once. Ansel has never seen an ocean, has never been in a boat.

It's a beautiful view. A man could die happy after such a sight.

Ansel does.

ONYX

ARGUS

What did you think of me? When you first saw me.
 Well, I thought you were beautiful.
 Really?
I thought, She has beautiful hair.
My hair. What about my eyes?
At first I couldn't see them. Not through your hair.
But then you did.
But then I did.
What did you think?
I thought, She has lovely eyes.
You did not.
I did. I really did.
Do you still think so?
I do. I always will.

Always is a very long time. It's the longest time.

It could never be long enough for me.

You're sweet. Do you think that will ever happen?

Do I think what will happen? Us? Always?

Yes. Us, for always.

It could. I think it could happen.

Don't you think you'd get tired of me? Everyone gets bored with everyone else.

I would be grateful for every moment, forever.

Grateful to who?

I don't know. To the universe.

That's easy to say now.

It's easy to say things that are true.

But you think you mean it.

I know I mean it.

Do you think that in one hundred years we'll remember this?

This conversation?

This. The conversation. You, there. Me, here. Us, together.

I think we'll still be having this conversation.

I'm going to pretend you meant that in a nice way.

I did. I meant it in the most wonderful way.

～ର～

The young man stares quietly through the window. He stands with his hands in his pockets. His shoulders are tired and slump a little. The satchel over his left shoulder scoots down a little. Without thinking about it, he pushes the strap back up. His knees are bent, as if he's being pressed down by some unseen thumb.

He sighs.

In the glass he can see the reflection of people milling around him. Most of them are doing just what he's doing: staring out into the dark.

Beside him, an old man in a sweater stands next to a little girl. He holds the girl's hand. The girl holds a rich orange gerbera daisy in her other hand. The vibrant color reminds the young man of autumn on the island.

◦◦◦

*T*here you are.

Good morning.

I don't know why I thought you would be anywhere else. It's so pretty here.

I like to watch the fog peel away from the water in the morning.

You're even literary when you talk. I like that.

Is that for me?

I made two cups. They're both for me.

Funny girl.

Silly man. I'm glad you brought me here. It's gorgeous. The leaves are starting to fall.

My grandparents used to bring me here when I was small. It was always cooler here than on the mainland. I used to run around on the lawn and kick through the leaves. There was almost always a steep wind off the water, so the leaves would sort of tornado around me, like they were trying to get away.

Did they live here?

My grandparents?

Yes.

No. They lived in northern California, just where the rolling hills turned to scrub. But Grandpa had a friend — from the war, I think — who owned this place, and let them use it once a year. Almost always in the fall.

How many times did you come?

Oh, I don't remember. The first time they brought me here, I think I was seven. Maybe eight. The last time was the year I was a junior in high school. The year Grandma died.

Do you miss her?

I do. I miss them both.

You brought me here. That's pretty special.

I tried to think of the most wonderful place.

There's no place more wonderful?

Not on Earth.

Ah, so there are possibilities.

Even if there are, I wouldn't care. You can't argue with this place.

It does have a special pull.

That's exactly what it has.

Like a gravitational force.

Sure. I guess.

The old man elbows him.

At first the younger man ignores this. There are enough people around the windows that he has been jostled several times already.

But then the old man elbows him again, and the younger man turns.

The old man smiles broadly, all teeth. He raises the little girl's hand and nods at it, then leans in and says, Do you think she appreciates this? Do you think she can even understand how precious this moment is?

The younger man rocks forward on his toes and looks at the girl more closely. She stares through the glass with a blank expression. Her hands are content to be still. Her fingers don't so much as twirl the stem of the daisy that rests against her collarbone. She's precious herself, small and delicate in a knee-length polka-dotted dress and dark shoes with tiny buckles. Her strawberry-blonde hair frames her freckled face in ringlets.

She's seven, the old man says.

When I was seven, I'm not sure I would have, the younger man says.

The old man frowns at this, then reconsiders, and smiles once more. But you're not seven now. You and I, I think we recognize this moment for what it is. You're a young buck, but I think you know.

I'm old enough, the younger man says.

So am I, the old man agrees. I've waited a very long time to see this. Now that it's here, I'm too interested in what other people think I think about it to feel the way I think I feel about it.

What other people?

The old man waves dismissively at the crowd that mills around them. Eh, he grunts. They're just people. Strangers, the whole lot of them. I take your point. I shouldn't let it bother me.

The younger man turns back to the window. Outside it is a starless night. The Earth is somewhere below, the moon somewhere behind. One of them casts a pale pool of light on the approaching wall, but he cannot tell which. Mae would have known.

Looming large in the window is the enormous crystalline flower of the space station, its petals cast open to reveal an interior of glittering spires and complex geometric structures. These are visible only for a moment, and then the shuttle passes below the station's horizon line. The beautiful surface modules disappear, and all the younger man can see are shuttle bays, dozens of them marked with reflective panels and pulsing caution lights.

This is so exciting, the old man says. I've waited so long for this moment.

The younger man grunts.

The old man looks at him with surprise. Not you?

The younger man says, Not particularly. No.

The old man opens his mouth to reply, but is interrupted before he can begin. The little girl tugs at his hand.

Grandpa, she says. I'm sleepy.

Okay, sweetheart, the old man says.

He crouches next to her and opens his arms. Up?

She nods, and steps into his embrace, resting her head on his shoulder. The old man closes his arms around her, tucks her knees in, and struggles to stand up.

The younger man offers a hand.

The old man grips it fiercely and pulls. The younger man did not expect such force, and locks his elbow and draws the old man to his feet.

Thank you, the old man says.

The girl stares obliquely into the distance as the old man gently sways.

The younger man returns his gaze to the window. The slow acceleration towards the docking bays has halted. Another much smaller shuttle drifts into view, adjusting tiny attitude jets to propel it gently into a lower bay. He watches it settle into place and sink on its broad duck feet.

The old man says, I didn't mean to offend you before.

The younger man turns. No offense. Really.

How impolite of me, the old man says. I should remember that not everybody cares what I think.

Not at all, says the younger man. Truly.

The old man regards him carefully, then adjusts his granddaughter in his arms and extends one hand. I'm Bernard, he says.

Micah, says the younger man.

Micah, the old man repeats.

◦⌒◦

Bernard nods in Micah's direction as the shuttle empties. Micah waits at the window a little longer, until the stream of passengers spills across the deck below like a box of brightly-colored candies. He is not entirely sure what he had expected from the journey, but so far it reminds him of little so much as a cattle car.

When he steps onto the landing platform, he pauses to collect himself. His fellow passengers, most of them, have swarmed to the processing checkpoints, where attendees in glass cubicles study and stamp paperwork and wave people on to their new homes. But a few mill about, perhaps waiting for the dishearteningly long processing lines to dwindle. Micah looks for a familiar face and sees none, though there is a middle-aged man standing next to a baggage trolley, alone.

Micah adjusts his satchel and starts to walk towards the stranger. He doesn't really want to talk to the man, but he also feels uncomfortable here, disconnected from other people among a crowd of partners and posses.

An electronic squeal bursts from the shuttle, and the passengers jump and stare up at the shuttle in alarm.

A voice says, NO DALLYING, PLEASE.

Micah cringes. It's louder than any voice he's ever heard, and he remembers what rock concerts were like, once. He casts about, looking for the owner of the voice, and spies him, a tiny, rotund man in an administrator's uniform and white cap.

The little man speaks into his hand again. PLEASE CONTINUE TO THE ARRIVALS PROCESSING CHECKPOINT IMMEDIATELY.

As his fellow passengers grumble and fall into line, Micah catches the administrator's eye.

He offers a small wave and a smile.

The administrator cocks his head, then, quite slowly, raises one small, gloved hand.

~◦~

Micah stands at the end of the line, alone. Ahead of him, the trail of passengers winds forward like a knot of licorice, uneven and clumped in places. He reaches into his pocket and plucks out a small gray card. It glimmers slightly. Its corners are rounded beads of fine glass. The card is blank save for a tiny engraved rectangle on the back.

He doesn't want it.

The line moves at a glacial pace. Micah takes advantage of this to look around. There's nothing particularly remarkable about this, his first close look at the interior of a space station. The landing deck is vast, and his shuttle is not the only one that has landed here to deposit its human payload. Micah squints and counts three more shuttles. The space between each is easily a quarter mile. He thinks about how many shuttle bays he saw during the approach — there were probably fifty or more.

He approximates the math. If each shuttle bay is a mile wide and half as deep, and there are fifty bays...

He blinks. The station is even larger than he had imagined.

Ahead, there is a disturbance in the line. He can hear scuffling and raised voices. He takes a step to his left to get a better view, and sees an administrator in a red uniform and white gloves. The administrator is waving his hands at the people in line, several of whom look like they might revolt.

I understand your frustration, the administrator is saying.

It's not easy to hear, but Micah watches anyway. The crowd pushes against him. A woman leans in close and shouts something at the administrator, who takes a step back and speaks into his wrist. Micah sees movement at the periphery of his vision and turns to see several more people in uniforms rushing to the administrator's aid.

Within moments, the uniformed newcomers have quelled the crowd. The administrator speaks to one man in particular, and that man steps out of line.

The man is immaculately and expensively dressed. His hair is perfectly coiffed, and he stands straight and tall and confident.

The man is holding a small gray card.

Micah puts his own card back into his pocket.

The administrator takes the man's bag from him and escorts him away from the line. Micah watches as they approach a series of freestanding clear tubes.

The administrator stops in front of one of the tubes. The tube stretches upward to the ceiling, which itself seems to be many miles away, its detail hazy and obscured by distance. The bottom of the tube rotates, and Micah can see that there is an outer and an inner layer. These rotate in opposite directions until they align, revealing an opening wide enough for the administrator and his guest to step through.

The tube's layers rotate again, sealing the two men inside. A moment later, the men are levitated upward.

Micah and his fellow passengers watch the two men float higher within the tube. Then they disappear through the ceiling, two small packages whisked away to some unknown destination.

Micah fingers the card inside of his pocket dubiously.

Lucky bastard, someone says.

He's not the only one, says another.

She's correct. Administrators are scuttling up and down the passenger lines like beetles. Here and there they pry a passenger out of line. Each of these selected passengers are well-dressed.

Each bears a small gray card.

～⊙～

*W*ould you ever want to live someplace else?
I don't know. I like it here.
I know. And it's beautiful. But what about someplace equally beautiful?

You aren't happy here?

I am. Of course I am. Micah — I am.

Is there someplace you want to go? Morocco or someplace?

Well...

There is. And it's better than this? Better than the ocean and the orange trees and the rain?

Micah, this place is lovely. I'm so happy you brought me here.

But you want to leave.

I don't know why we can't just have a conversation.

Alright. Fine. Let's talk about it.

Not like this. It's not even important. It's not even real. Forget about it.

I can't forget about it. Clearly this is important to you.

Micah —

Well, where is it? France? Australia?

Micah.

Belgium? Maybe Portugal is a nicer place than this.

You're being cruel.

I'm not. Tell me where.

It's none of those places. It's not important.

Italy?

Micah.

Is it Italy?

No, it's not Italy.

Alright. Which direction from Italy?

Micah. Jesus.

Which direction?

Up.

What? Up?

Up.

Okay. Alaska. Greenland.

Up.

The Arctic Circle. That's got to be it. You want to live on an icebreaker ship, saving polar bears. That's obviously better than here.

Up.

The North Pole.

More up.

There's no more up you can go!

You're not listening to me. You never listen when you get like this.

Look, the North Pole is the top. There's no more up.

You weren't listening.

All I do is listen to you!

I didn't say north, asshole. I said up.

~⚬~

ernard and his granddaughter are somewhere in the middle of the line. The girl is still on his shoulder, but sleeping now.

Micah falls out of the line and quickly walks to where the old man is standing.

Hey, someone says.

Micah turns and, walking backward, says, No, no, I'm not jumping the line. It's okay.

He reaches Bernard and puts his hand on the old man's shoulder. Bernard, he says.

Bernard turns. He is sweating profusely.

Micah, the old man says.

Are you okay?

Bernard nods at the girl. She is not a little bird any more. But she is tired, and so for now, I will hold her as long as I can.

It's a long line, though, Micah says.

You are an astute observer, Bernard replies, not without some sarcasm.

I brought you something, Bernard. Here.

Bernard's eyebrows raise. Oh?

Here, Micah repeats.

Bernard looks down and sees Micah's hand holding a gray card. The old man's eyes widen. What are you doing, Micah? he asks. Do you know what that is?

Sort of, Micah says.

You don't have to be here, man. Go!

Bernard turns, looking about for an administrator.

Micah grabs his shoulder. No, he says. I want you to take it.

Bernard jostles the woman ahead of him in line. She whirls about.

I'm sorry, Bernard says. But the woman's irritation is defused by the card she sees in Micah's hand.

Dear god, she says. You have a card? You have a card!

No, Micah says. No, it's —

Who has a card? someone else says.

This man here has a card, the woman says.

Micah turns back to Bernard. I want you to have this, he says. Please.

He tries to push the card into Bernard's hand, but the old man snatches his hand away. What are you doing? Micah!

Take it, Micah repeats.

It is too much, Bernard protests. It is too valuable. I can't.

Give it to me, the woman interrupts, reaching for the card.

Micah turns away from her. It's not for you, he says.

If you're giving it away, I want it, someone else says.

Micah presses the card into Bernard's hand again. Please. It would help you.

The line begins to come apart around the two men. Strangers surge into the gaps, pushing.

I'll take it! someone shouts.

Give it to me!

I must have it! It would change my baby's life!

Please!

Me!

Give it!

Micah takes advantage of the commotion to close Bernard's fingers around the card. The old man looks confused to find the card in his hand, and Micah tries to melt away in the mob of passengers.

What's happening here? a deep voice booms.

Instantly the crowd begins to dissolve, and Micah sees one of the red-suited administrators stalking towards him. He's carrying a baton in one hand.

Nothing, someone says.

Everything's fine!

I didn't do it!

It's not mine!

The administrator spies the card in Bernard's hand. His gaze shifts to Bernard's worried face, then back to the card.

Sir, the administrator says to Bernard.

It's not his card, someone snitches.

The administrator turns toward the passengers behind Bernard, then looks back at Bernard. Is this true? Is this your card?

Bernard is petrified. His granddaughter starts awake, her face flushed.

Grandpa? she says, her voice fuzzy with sleep.

Sir? Is that card yours?

Bernard holds up the card, unable to find his voice.

It's mine, Micah says, stepping forward.

Bernard's entire body relaxes, and the card falls to the floor.

The administrator puts the toe of his boot on the card. He studies Micah's face carefully, then his attire.

This card belongs to you? he asks Micah.

Micah nods. It does.

This man did not steal it from you? The administrator indicates Bernard with his baton.

Bernard tenses at the sight of the stick pointed in his direction.

Micah reaches out and tips the baton toward the floor. The administrator steps back quickly.

Absolutely he didn't steal it, Micah says. I wanted to give it to him.

The administrator looks suspicious. You wanted to give him your Onyx card.

Bernard finds his voice. I didn't try to take it!

Onyx cards are not transferable, the administrator says sternly.

I didn't want it! Bernard cries.

I didn't know that, Micah says.

I find that difficult to believe, the administrator says. Every Onyx cardholder knows that the card is not transferable.

I didn't, Micah says. I inherited it from my wife.

From your wife, the administrator echoes.

She's gone, Micah says. I wanted to give the card away.

Bernard looks at Micah. His expression changes. All of his alarm and tension vanishes, and in its place is a look of such pure compassion that Micah has to turn away. He knows that look. He's seen it before, on other faces. On the faces of people who have lost people. On the faces of people who still feel the prick of loss every morning when they turn over in bed.

It doesn't really work that way, sir, the administrator says.

I didn't know that.

It's alright, the administrator says. Then he turns his mouth into his wrist and says something that Micah doesn't quite hear.

Micah glances at Bernard, who is still looking at

him with those terribly sad eyes.

It's okay, Micah mouths at him.

Bernard shakes his head sadly and mouths something back that looks like, So young.

Then an escort in a soft gray uniform arrives, and the administrator says to Micah, Please, allow Mr. Hedderly to take your bag.

The escort smiles at Micah. His teeth are impossibly white. Every last one of them is perfectly placed and perfectly visible. May I, sir?

Micah sighs and looks at Bernard, and then at the administrator. Couldn't I just stay in line?

Behind him, a woman says, He did *not* just say that.

I'm afraid not, sir, the administrator says. May I?

He holds his hand out for the card.

Micah gives it to him.

Your thumb, sir.

The administrator turns the card over to reveal the rectangle printed there.

Micah sighs again, then presses his thumb down on the rectangle. The card lights up, and Mae's face appears on its surface. Her name, identification code, and physical attributes are drawn in beside it.

Mae Isabella Atherton-Sparrow
0522FG010-EPG
H 5'3"   W 112

Micah stares at the photograph of Mae. He

remembers the day that they visited the Settlement Transition Bureau. They had fought that day. He hadn't wanted to go, which was usually enough to deter Mae. That day had been different. She had gone anyway, without telling him, and it wasn't until weeks later that he found the Onyx card in her bag while he was looking for the chocolates she often kept hidden there. He had been angry.

The photograph was perhaps the most beautiful picture of Mae he had ever seen. It was low-quality, with artifacts that interrupted the image. Like most global agencies, the STB didn't spend much on equipment. It didn't matter how bad the photograph itself was. The image of Mae that shone through was beautiful because of her expression.

It was the purest expression of happiness and hope. Her eyes were alive, brighter and larger than life. Her smile stretched wider than he had imagined possible, shoving her round cheeks high. Her skin was flushed, as if she couldn't believe what was happening, couldn't contain her excitement.

He had never seen her so happy before.

∽⊚∾

Y*ou don't mean —*
    Yes. Up.
    Up.
Yes.
I can't.

You have to admit it would be beautiful.

But I... I. Up?

Up, Micah. Up there. It would be beautiful, too. Not like this, but beautiful in other ways. Beautiful because it would mean something... more.

It's a million miles away.

Well, no. It's not.

Fine, okay. Not a million, but it might as well be. Jesus, Mae.

I didn't know you felt strongly about it.

I feel strongly about Earth! Under my feet! I like standing here. Do you know who built this pier? No? Well, I do. His name was Marcus Perrine, and he was twenty-eight when he built it with his bare hands as a gift for his bride. It's been here for nearly eighty years. There's history here. I like history.

There's history there, too. More history, even.

Don't be ridiculous. It's not the same.

You really wouldn't? For me?

I'm not a spaceman, Mae.

You wouldn't even think about it?

I'm from Earth. What's up there that isn't here? Don't scientists spend their careers looking for places just like Earth? Why do you think that is? It's because its Earths that matter. They're rare and precious and beautiful and amazing. And I like living here. It smells nice. It makes my heart happy.

Not even for me?

Mae.

Micah.

You're asking so much.

It would be the grandest adventure. It would be thrilling

every day.

No, it wouldn't. It would be terribly boring.

I've dreamed of going there since they built the first one. Galileo. I was eight.

You've dreamed of moving to space since you were eight years old.

Yes! Yes, Micah. I wanted to watch the sun rise.

What do you think we just watched?

Not here, Micah. To watch the sun rise over the entire planet. I want to float! I want to float like a feather. I want to —

You want to live in a dark cold scary vacuum that will kill you.

Yes. I do, I do! Because we tamed it, Micah. Look what we did! Look up, you can even see them up there now.

I don't want to look up.

Now you're just being petulant.

Living in orbit would make me miserable.

How do you —

Some things you just know. You just do.

You really wouldn't even consider it?

What about our families, Mae? What about Christmases and Thanksgivings and birthdays?

Maybe they'll all come with us. Who knows! Don't you think being a part of something greater than yourself is worth missing a few family holidays?

Not a few, Mae. All of them. Or didn't you know that you can't come back?

I knew it.

So, really, you're okay with leaving our families forever. Is that what they mean to you?

You're missing the point, Micah.

Oh, am I.

I've always wondered what an impasse feels like.

Don't be dramatic.

Well, what would you call it?

So we're doomed, is that it? Because I don't want to be a spaceman with you?

Don't make light.

Look. Mae. I love you. You know I do.

I need a few minutes.

You know I'd do anything for you.

Micah, give me a minute. Okay?

I should go inside?

Forget it. I will.

Wait. Mae, wait.

❧

T he image of Mae and her details disappear from the card. A simple red line of text appears in its place.

Deceased January 7 2178

The administrator glances up at Micah, then back down at the card. He touches it with two fingers, and the red text disappears. A single small dot dances on the card. The administrator says, Inheritor.

Micah blinks, only now realizing that his eyes are

damp.

The blinking dot vanishes, and a new profile appears. Where the photo should be, there is a simple empty box.

Micah Roderick Sparrow
0627J007-1211-E
H 5'11"   W 192

You can remove your thumb now, the administrator says. Stand up straight, Mr. Sparrow.

The administrator holds the card at Micah's eye level. The surface of the card reflects Micah's face back at him. He is startled to see that he has two long tear-streaks on his skin, and he quickly wipes them away with the heels of his palms.

Big smile, the administrator says. One. Two. Three. Snap!

The image on the card freezes.

The administrator turns the card over and looks at the image, then up at Micah. Maybe one more try? he says.

Micah shakes his head.

The image is the exact opposite of Mae's. Micah's expression is one of a lost soul.

Unlike Mae's beautiful smile, Micah has seen this expression on his face every day for two years.

Mr. Sparrow, says the escort in the gray suit. Shall we?

Micah looks at Bernard. I'm sorry, he says.

Bernard nods. Me, too.

I meant —

I know what you meant. Be well, Micah.

The escort takes the Onyx card from the administrator and returns it to Micah.

Micah absently tucks it into his pocket.

Mr. Sparrow, the administrator says, extending his hand. Welcome to Argus Station.

ONYX

*W*hat are you doing?

Reading. You're in my light.

Maybe we should talk about this.

I don't want to.

It's important that we work these things out. Otherwise what are we?

I don't want to talk about it, Micah.

Mae.

Leave me alone.

What are you reading?

Leave me alone, please.

We'll talk about it later.

Whatever.

Micah stares at his reflection in the mirror. He is older than he remembers. He has crows' feet on either side of his tired brown eyes. When he concentrates, it looks like someone has pulled a rake across his forehead. There are fault lines, deep ones, framing his mouth. The effect is that his face looks as if it has been assembled from several pieces. He forces an inauthentic smile and watches the lines deepen and shift.

He sighs, and bends over the sink and splashes water on his face.

The sun has broken over the Earth since he last looked outside. The view from his apartment makes him ill. He pads barefoot across the chamber to a window that spans the entire exterior wall, from the floor of his apartment to the high ceiling. The glass is deeply tinted, but the orange glow that suffuses the city below is powerful all the same.

He touches the glass with all five fingers, then rotates his hand slightly to his right. A faint contrail appears beneath his fingers. Above it is a readout: 90/100. As he turns his hand, the number climbs, and the window darkens measurably. He turns his hand to the left. The number falls to 74/100, and Micah has to close his eyes against the fierce brightness that the weaker shade has revealed.

He rotates his hand to the right blindly until his eyelids are no longer shot through with angry red darts. For a while after he opens them again, his vision is imprinted with slashes of red that turn white and disappear after a few seconds.

He squeezes his eyes shut tightly, then flexes his fingers as wide as they will go. He holds this stretching position until his hands tremble, then exhales slowly, relaxing the muscles in his hands just as slowly. When he has relaxed completely, his hands are like soggy hunks of bread, invisible in the tactile spectrum of nerves that make up his identity.

The apartment would please anybody. Three thousand square feet, richly furnished, with a floor that absorbs his weight and is so soft that he could sleep on it if he chose. The bed is positioned in such a way that he will wake to a view of Argus City each morning, with its spires and towering spacescrapers and humming air traffic. The walls are designed in moveable sets, so that Micah can adjust the apartment's layout to suit his needs.

He has no interest in the floor plan.

Micah rotates his hand on the window until it becomes opaque. The window vanishes, its interior surface now the same color as the apartment's walls.

If desired, I can apply some digital art to these walls, a voice says.

I don't desire, Micah says.

He crosses the room to the bed.

Shall I adjust the climate to complement your resting body temperature?

Do whatever you want, Micah says.

He stretches out in the bed, grips one of the spare pillows as if it is another warm body, and tries to sleep.

The escort in the gray suit had had plenty to say about Micah's new environment. After their stomach-turning ride through the giant transport tubes, during which Micah had watched a dozen decks full of new arrivals zoom by, the escort had given Micah a brief tour.

Don't you have other visitors to meet? Micah had asked, annoyed.

Oh, no, the escort replied. Each Onyx resident has a dedicated escort for their first week. After that week, the escorts are less vital, and more of a convenience. There are usually four of us for each petal floor.

How many residents are on each floor?

Approximately two hundred, the escort answered.

And how many floors?

Each petal has five hundred floors. There are ten petals altogether, he added.

Micah was surprised. The station seems like it could support more than just a million people, he said. That's only a tenth of the population of most of the big cities in America.

The escort nodded. This way, he said.

Micah followed the escort across a grand lobby. At the nearest end, the lobby looked into the heart of Argus City. He stopped and stared for a moment, his eyes following one canyon between the tall buildings as far as he could, until the city faded into a blue haze and lost all definition.

How far across is the city? he asked.

Two hundred forty miles, sir.

Two hundred forty miles of city for just one million people? That seems... wasteful.

The escort shook his head. Oh, no, sir. One million is the number of Onyx residents, but Onyx-class residents are just a small percentage of Argus's total occupancy.

I don't understand, Micah said.

On the arrival deck, the escort said. All of the other new arrivals? Your fellow passengers on the shuttle?

Micah remembered.

Well, sir, they comprise the Machine-class residents.

Machine-class?

Machine-class, the escort repeated. As in, they are the machine that keeps Station Argus going.

I don't understand, Micah said again.

Don't worry, the escort said, striking off toward another series of lift tubes. Everything will be explained.

※

Where were you this afternoon?
Out.
Mae, can we stop being so hostile?
I'm not being hostile. That's where I was. Out.
This is so exhausting.
I don't know what's so exhausting about it.
This.
This what?

This whole argument. It's... it's seeping into who we are.

I don't know what you mean.

Yes, you do. Look, I know you want to go to space. Okay? I know. I'm sorry that I don't.

It's not that simple. And I don't want to talk about it.

We have to talk about it. We have to get past this.

No, Micah. No, we don't. We can't.

Can't?

You really don't understand this, do you.

Understand what? We both have things that we wish we could do that we won't ever get to do.

Well, thanks for deciding for me.

Come on, Mae.

Don't patronize me.

It feels like this isn't going to get better.

You just want me to put this back in the box I took it out of. I know what you want, Micah. You want what you always get. You want your way.

That's not what I want.

It is! And it's what you always get, too. It's the idea of my having dreams that you like. You think it makes me adorable and interesting. But it's the reality of my having dreams that you hate, because it might upend your happy routine.

Jesus. Mae, is that what you think?

I don't have to think it, Micah. It's obvious.

I don't hate the idea of you having dreams.

You missed the point. That's not what I said. You hate the reality of my having dreams.

I don't, either.

Then I want to go to space. And I want you to come

with me, Micah. As my husband, the man who I want to build a future with. Come with me! We'll raise our family there, and our children will grow up at the changing, exciting edge of history. They'll tell their children one day, and their grandchildren, that they were raised in space, one of the first couple of generations to do it. They'll be like the pioneers who set out for California, or the first immigrants to America. Let's go, Micah. Let's go to space and look down at the Earth and up at the stars. They'll be closer than ever, almost close enough to touch. Let's be there when we get tired of living in orbit, and we decide it's time to go wherever is next. We'll be old then, but we can say, Wow, look at humanity go! Look at how far we've —

Mae, I don't want to live in space. I want to live right here, in this house on this shore with this view and this rain and this creaky old pier and these trees. I want our kids to plant their own trees in this yard and watch them grow to a hundred feet tall. I want them to carve little notches in the door frames each year to see how much they've grown. I want them to fill this house with a lifetime of our things so that one day there's this pleasant clutter that we'll always find some memory buried in. I want a happy and long life right here, Mae. And I want you with me.

I know all of that, Micah. And don't worry. You'll win. You'll get to have all of that.

Mae, come on —

No. No, that's what you want. I know. You want me to sulk for a couple of days, then get over it, and we'll get old and wrinkly and pretend that there was never a time when we fought about this. You might actually forget about it for real.

In fact, I know you will. That's what you do. You've got one big-ass rug in your brain, Micah, and you're really good at sweeping shit under it that you never want to see again.

Mae, please —

No! No, that's what's going to happen. You'll be this oblivious, cheerful old man, and all of our grandchildren will love you because you're so happy, because you're living the perfect life you've always dreamed of, and every day is just a vacation for you. And they'll have less of a connection with me, because they'll know, somehow, somewhere deep inside, that something isn't quite right about Grandma. They won't know what it is, but they'll be able to tell, because when a person has a dream that they've dreamed of their whole life, and they don't get a single chance to accomplish it in the single life that belongs to them, they just sort of wither inside, Micah, they dry up and rot on the inside, and the nice thing is that nobody can see it on the outside, not really well, so everybody else can pretend that everything is okay. But not me, Micah. I'll get the great pleasure of dying a little inside every single day that you get to have the life you want, and I have to put my own dreams in a fucking box and fucking burn it.

∽⊛∾

Y ou're on the eighty-fifth floor, the escort had said. I hope you're not afraid of heights. And if you are, just imagine two things. First, remember that there are four hundred fifteen floors that are even higher than yours.

And second? Micah asked.

Oh, just that you're already thirty thousand miles above the place where you were born, the escort said cheerfully.

That's reassuring, Micah said. Is it really thirty thousand miles?

Thirty-two thousand miles, six hundred feet. Or something like that.

Huh, Micah said. Hey, before — before you said that everything would be explained. You know that my Onyx card isn't actually mine, right?

You inherited it, the escort said. Right. Don't worry about that. We have quite a few inheritors. It's not unusual to inherit an Onyx card without having taken the classes.

There are classes?

Oh, yes. Every Onyx-class candidate takes a twelve-week course on Earth after they're identified.

What sort of classes? Micah had asked.

Oh, everything from what to expect from an artificial-grav environment to how to interact effectively with an A.I. to a history series about the stations, the escort said. Pretty basic orientation stuff, really.

So what do, um, inheritors do to learn this stuff?

I'll introduce you to your A.I., the escort said. Let's zip up to your floor, then.

My A.I.? Micah had asked.

Sure. It'll be great, don't worry.

Do I have to have an A.I.? What if I just want to be alone?

Oh, that's the best part, the escort said. You just tell the A.I. to go away. Just say, Bob, I'd like to be alone. And there you go.

Bob?

Well, you can name yours whatever you want. I'm sure somebody chose Bob for theirs.

But not you?

Oh, I don't have an A.I., Mr. Sparrow.

You don't? Micah asked. Why not? That seems unfair.

I'm Machine-class, sir, the escort said.

Machine-class.

It's grand, sir, the escort said cheerfully. Your A.I. will teach you all about it. I'm sure you'll enjoy it.

Machine-class, Micah repeated.

Yes, sir. Let's take the lift now, shall we?

And up they went.

⚬⚬⚬

I *don't think you should go.*

It's not up to you.

Maybe. I guess. But I wish you wouldn't.

This is kind of serious, Micah. It's a good opportunity for me at work. If I do well, it might change the way they perceive me. Who knows, it could turn into a promotion, even.

I don't like you going away when we're in the middle of a fight.

I don't like fighting with you, Micah.

I don't like fighting with you, either. We should just call a cease-fire. Truce.

That only works when it's not an important fight. It won't work for this.

What if you don't come back?

Is that what you're afraid of?

I'm afraid you won't come back.

I'll come back. Even if it's just to get my stuff.

That's not funny.

I know.

Are you serious?

I think a little break will put things in perspective, Micah. But it's not going to change my point.

Then why take a break? We'll be in the same place then that we are now.

Because I'm tired of sleeping badly because we're both all worked-up over this. It'll be good for us. You need the break, too.

I don't. I don't want it.

Micah, it's just two weeks. I'm going to be working. You'll be working. We'll hardly notice it.

I'll notice it.

Micah.

I will. I'll come home to this place, empty. You'll go home to a fancy hotel, probably nice dinners with your boss, who knows what.

Don't imply anything. That's not going to help.

I'm sorry. I can't help it. I'm a wreck thinking about you leaving.

You'll have this place to yourself again. You love it here. It'll be good for you.

I don't want it to myself.

Micah. Make the most of the two weeks. Think about something else. Work on a project.

I could build the crib. The one we talked about.

Don't do that.

What? Why not?

Micah, don't do that. You know what you're doing. Don't do that. Build a bookcase or something.

Shit. You aren't coming back, are you. You're really not coming back, and you already know it. You're just dragging this out. Well, if that's what you're going to do, then do it. Rip it off, Mae. Do it.

Micah, it's a work trip. I'm coming back.

You don't want me to build the crib.

You're just being awful to yourself if you build it, Micah. We aren't ready for kids and won't be any time soon. We have real things to figure out here.

I can't believe that moving to space is the thing we have to figure out. I can't believe moving to space is the thing that might ruin us.

Well, that's a problem. You even treat the idea of this problem like a joke.

Oh, I didn't mean it like that, Mae. I —

I think you did. Look, I'm going to pack. We can talk a bit more tonight, and in the morning I have to fly out. My flight is at six, so I'll be gone early.

Where's the trip to?

Tokyo.

Where are you staying?

I don't know. I have the itinerary somewhere. You can have a copy, okay? But Micah, I want to treat this like a time-out. I don't want to talk to you every night. I don't want to hear about your day. I want time to think about our future without you putting your foot in your mouth.

I can't even call?

Look. I love you. I have always loved you, and I always will, no matter what. But Micah, you think that my biggest, most life-long dream is a farce, and you're standing in the way of me ever even having a chance to accomplish it. So yes, we have things to figure out, and no, I don't want to talk to you for a little while.

I don't think it's a farce.

Micah —

Say whatever you want, Mae. I don't think it's a farce. It just... scares me.

Alright, we're done.

Hey —

No. Every time we fight, if there's a real problem we can't work out, you play-act this emotional psychobabble moment of discovery, like you've just come to terms with something about yourself. But it's a goddamn trick, Micah. I'm supposed to see how vulnerable you are, and come running to you and comfort you. But it's just a diversion. I don't even think you know you're doing it. But I'm going upstairs to pack, and we can talk about this in two weeks when I come home and we've both had time to really think about what we want to do next.

I don't do that. Mae? I don't do that. Mae, come on.

~⚬~

Micah starts awake to a blinding light. He turns over in bed, throws his arm over his eyes.

The window is transparent again.

He says, What the hell?

The A.I. speaks up. You were in your optimum sleep state for waking, Micah. Gradual light is a positive way to emerge from a restful state.

Gradual, hell. Close the window.

As you wish, Micah.

The window becomes opaque again.

❦

Hours later Micah awakes on his own. The apartment is completely dark. He rolls over and swings his feet over the edge of the bed.

You are awake, the A.I. says. May I provide anything for you?

Don't talk to me when I wake up, Micah says. You can start with that.

Very well.

Micah pads into the kitchen, barefoot. The floor is almost spongy beneath his feet. As much as he misses the water-logged planks of the pier back home, he must admit that this is nice.

He touches the door of the pantry. It hisses open like an airlock. Micah frowns. He misses the old tacky sound of his refrigerator opening. Everything in the apartment sounds like a television show's idea of the future. He looks around for a toaster but doesn't see one. If there was one, it would probably sound like a ray gun.

The pantry is empty. Micah goes around the kitchen, opening panels one by one. There's nothing inside. The cooling closet is empty as well.

A.I., he says, finally.

Yes, Micah.

I think I need to buy food. I don't know how to do that.

Micah, if you'll join me in the dining space, I'll be pleased to explain how to acquire food, the A.I. says.

Your speech is weird, Micah says as he walks into the dining room.

Define weird, the A.I. replies.

The voice seems to emerge from the air. There are no visible speakers in the apartment, and the A.I. has no visible avatar or physical body of any kind. It's simply... there.

Weird, Micah repeats. You know, oddly formal but sometimes not formal at all. It's like a blend of two completely different cultures.

Let's select a voice pattern that you'll identify with, the A.I. suggests. Please sit. Do you prefer a male voice, a female voice, or an androgynous voice?

Micah thinks about this. Female, he says, finally.

He hears three faint tones.

How's this? the A.I. says.

The almost sterile travel-guide voice of the A.I. has been replaced with that of a female.

Say something else, Micah says. Tell me about the weather.

Unfortunately, there is no natural weather in space, the A.I. says. I can tell you about the simulated weather events and the schedule by which they occur.

No, that's okay, Micah says. That's enough. How much can you modify the female voice?

You have several variables to select from, the A.I. says. You may modify the masculinity or femininity of my voice. You may select regional influences. You may adjust the formality or informality of my speech. You may even provide me with an input sample that I may mimic as closely as possible.

Micah considers this. Your voice is a little flat. Maybe it could sound a little, I don't know, warmer? More friendly.

Like this? the A.I. asks.

Say something else.

The simulated air flow adopts a weaving pattern through the city, carrying a pleasant breeze down each street, and modulating the —

That's enough, Micah says. That's better. Friendly-sounding but not too intimate.

If you would like to adjust for intimacy at a later time, you may modify my voice settings at your leisure, the A.I. says.

What do you mean by intimacy? Micah says.

There are multiple definitions of the word, the A.I. explains. You may adjust my properties for most of them. If you prefer me to address you in more personal ways, or assume a deeper history than we actually possess, then I can adjust my words to approximate that sort of intimacy. However, some users on the station prefer their A.I. to address them with content which is more intimate.

You mean they like their A.I.s to talk dirty to them, Micah says.

If by dirty you mean speech which has sexual or provocative content, then you are correct.

Isn't that a little — I don't know — low-tech? Weren't there people doing phone-sex routines like a hundred years ago?

It may be antiquated, but I understand that the human mind remains stimulated by imagery, whether that imagery is created with words or pictures.

We'll skip that part, Micah says. You sound more friendly, but your voice is still kind of bland.

Would you like to add a regional influence to my speech?

Micah thinks about this. How specific can I be?

You may select an influence as broad as a continent, or as narrow as a town or city. You may also adjust that influence by era. For example, if you prefer Victorian-era British speech, rather than twentieth century British speech, you may calibrate for such a preference.

What if you don't have the region I am interested in?

The A.I. says, I have access to a library of audio captures that are up to two hundred years old. I believe I can provide a reasonable solution if you select a region not represented in that catalog.

Okay, Micah says. Let's try California.

I have many California samples. Is there a preferred region?

Try the central coast area.

The central coast of California is available, with several further regional filters. Shall I list them?

Micah shrugs. Sure.

Monterey, California. Big Sur, California. Carmel-by-the-Sea, California. San Luis Obispo, California. Salinas, California. Santa Barbara, California. Montecito, California. San Simeon, California. Arroyo Grande, California. Morro Bay, California. Cayucos, California. Lompoc, California. Santa Cruz, California. Los Olivos, California. San—

That's enough. A lot of those areas are really close — are you sure there's much difference between them?

Every region has a minor differentiator from the regions that surround it, the A.I. says.

Okay.

Micah visited Mae in her hometown just once, returning with her for a family reunion. She had grown up in Morro Bay, a little seaside town shadowed by a large volcanic rock. He remembered liking it very much. It reminded him of the beach house and its gray ocean and chilly skies.

Morro Bay, California, he says to the A.I.

He hears three dim tones again.

Say something, he says.

The city of Morro Bay, California, is located on a waterfront in San Luis Obispo County, the A.I. says.

Can you raise the tone of your voice? Less deepness.

Three tones.

The A.I. continues. Morro Bay's population in the early twenty-first century was —

Stop. Jesus, stop.

Micah holds his hands out and looks at his arms. His skin is covered in goosebumps. His forehead has broken out in a cool sweat.

Shall I adjust the variables —

For god's sake shut the fuck up, Micah cries.

The A.I.'s voice is eerily, horribly similar to Mae's. Micah doesn't know what he was thinking. He pushes back from the table in a hurry and walks out of the room. Over his shoulder he says, Make a new adjustment. Pick a male voice, any goddamn male voice. Adjust!

Three tones.

The A.I.'s voice is present in the living quarters, where Micah has just walked to escape the awful simulacrum of Mae that he has just created, like some sort of monster-maker.

Is this better? the A.I. asks. The voice is gravelly, deep, emphatic.

It's perfect, Micah says, pulling at his hair. Accept. It's good. Use that.

Your final selection step is to choose a name, the A.I. says. I can provide you with any naming resources you —

Bob, Micah says. Your name is Bob.

Three tones.

Bob's your uncle, the A.I. says. A joke.

Don't joke with me, Micah says.

Three tones.

Adjustment complete. Humor will not be a feature of this selection.

Go away now, Micah says.

Very well, says the A.I., who sounds like a middle-aged smoker.

Micah goes back to the bed and wraps himself around the spare pillow again, and presses his face into its softness, and screams the longest scream he can sustain. Eyes red-rimmed and tender, pillow smushed against his cheek, he drifts into a terrible sleep.

MACHINE

Where would you like to begin? Bob asks. Micah is standing at the window, staring down at Argus City. It is nightfall, at least until the sun rises again in ninety minutes. He doesn't know how people adjust to the frequent sunrises. Maybe their windows are timed to the station's orbital schedule, and darken each time the sun breaks like a nuclear bomb over the city.

I don't care, Micah says. Do I really have to spend

twelve weeks learning this stuff?

Twelve weeks is the Earth course length, Bob says. You're already here. You can learn what you like when you like, on an as-needed or as-desired basis. Or you can simply walk the halls alone, a rogue gunslinger who doesn't need anything from anybody.

Adjust for drama, Bob, Micah grumbles.

Three tones.

What a shame, Bob says. I was good at it.

Where do you think I should start?

Bob says, Perhaps a history lesson. I can tell you how the station fleet came to be, when the first station was constructed in orbit, and describe the current status of all twelve stations.

Let me save you some time, Micah says. We poisoned the Earth, so we built floating boats in space. The first station was built fifty years ago, and now there are twelve, and this is the coolest one.

That's fairly accurate, Bob says.

Alright, then. Let's move on.

Perhaps we should begin with the Onyx designation, Bob suggests.

Micah flaps his hands restlessly in the pockets of his bathrobe. I don't want any pop quizzes or tests, he says. Isn't there a movie or something that you could show me instead?

Do you mean an instructional video, or a dramatic film that captures the essence of the topic?

Either, I guess.

Both exist, although the instructional video is

now a bit dated, and the dramatic films are usually melodramatic and feature stories of class divisions and unrequited love, Bob says.

You sound cynical, Bob.

I simply think that my summaries will prove more useful, Bob says. I can pare them down to shorter descriptions, if you like.

Short is good. I think I want to go back to sleep.

If I may, Bob says, you do sleep a —

You may not, Micah says.

Very well. Shall I begin?

Shoot.

∽⊚∾

The Onyx program, Bob begins, was created in 2182, just over a century after the first station, Station Ganymede, was deployed in high orbit. The first few years of Ganymede's progress proved interesting for sociologists, who discovered that the broad sample of humans who comprised the first space settlers were lost at sea.

Lost at sea?

Sociologically speaking, Bob says. If you recall, the first station was an experiment in class-leveling. Each person who was admitted to the first class of settlers was stripped of social status and assets. In short, each person began a new life as a perfect equal to the other settlers.

How extreme was it? Micah asks.

The most affluent member of the first settlement class was Harvey Bogleman. His personal fortune was about three hundred billion dollars when he signed up for admission. He left a small portion of the money to his family who remained on Earth, and donated the rest to the space settlement program.

That's one way to make sure you still see the benefit of your fortune, I guess, Micah says.

Indeed, Mr. Bogleman's donation accounted for approximately one-hundredth the cost of the second station, Cassiopeia. His donation, however, did not benefit him personally. He remained on Station Ganymede until his death in 2086. Having given up his privileged and wealthy status, he would have been mistaken if he had believed his donation to the program would have resulted in a better stateroom on a newer station.

Huh, Micah says. Alright, so what happened with the class experiment? It sounds like it failed.

It failed, Bob says. Sociologists concluded that humans accustomed to class perceptions found it quite difficult to shake their preconceived notions of their own status, or that of other settlers. Mr. Bogleman, in fact, fell prey to such difficulties. He was disciplined for creating an exclusive club for himself and a handful of other settlers. He called it the Harvard Club, in reference to the prestigious American institute.

So rich people still saw themselves as rich, and poor people still felt poor.

Put simply, yes. The Onyx program was created to

classify future settlers in two simple categories: Onyx settlers, and Machine settlers.

Why Onyx? I mean, why was it called that.

Surprisingly, that origin story is not preserved, Bob says. I suppose someone liked the word. However, the Machine-class designation has a clearer basis.

Yeah, the escort fellow told me, Micah says. I thought it was pretty discriminatory.

On the contrary, Bob says, the purpose was to create a simple, A-B class system in order to give all settlers a clear purpose. The clearer a person's understanding of their place in the system, the theory goes, the more productive and happy they are freed to be. However, others shared your view of the program.

That it discriminates? That it's a box for second-class citizens?

The program was debated and refined by a panel of experts. A majority rule shaped the program into its final incarnation. However, two panelists resisted the program forcefully, citing a belief that it would set human progress back by a thousand years.

My kind of people, Micah says. Who were they? The two dissenters.

The first was Marshall Onlin, who originally conceived of the Onyx program. He felt that the program had been significantly changed from its initial concept, and became vocally opposed to it. The second, Bob says, was Tasneem Kyoh, a cultural anthropologist who experienced the Ganymede social experiment first-hand.

But they lost, obviously.

Obviously, Bob agrees.

So who decides who is Machine-class and who isn't? Do people buy their way into the Onyx class? It can't be that, because my wife didn't have money.

Each prospective settler is given a series of tests to identify skills. Those with extremely high intelligence markings, critical thinking skills, visionary qualities and so forth are set aside for the Onyx class. The average applicant is more suited for positions that leverage their Earth-honed talents for manufacturing, maintenance, analysis, construction, service and other industries that permit broad ranges of aptitude, Bob says.

So the smart, charismatic people get special treatment, Micah says.

Essentially, Bob says. People with these qualities are generally quite suited for roles that benefit humanity in more resonant ways. For example, Onyx-class settlers are permitted to participate in station government and have a voice in fleet planning and futures.

I don't like this, Micah says. This sounds like you're isolating people in big buckets marked Best and Worst.

That's a simple and misinformed understanding, Bob says. Many people in the Machine class share that view.

I'm not surprised. What other privileges do Onyx people get?

Perhaps the most prominent benefit is reproductive freedom, Bob says.

～☙～

Reproductive freedom? You're shitting me. Onyx-class citizens are permitted to reproduce with other Onyx citizens at their leisure. Monogamous relationships are actively discouraged, Bob explains.

Who decided this? Micah says.

The fleet council made this a key component of the Onyx program in the fourteenth revision to the bylaws.

Fleet council, Micah says.

That's correct. The fleet council is comprised of five representatives from each of the twelve stations.

What about Machine-class citizens?

What about them? Bob asks.

What about their rights to reproduce? This is insane. I can't believe I have to ask this question.

Your questions are within the boundaries of our topic, Bob says.

That's not what I mean. I should have fucking taken that class. I shouldn't be here.

To answer your previous question, Machine-class citizens are permitted to reproduce when and if they successfully win the annual lottery, Bob says.

Micah whirls away from the window. There's a goddamn lottery?

Two hundred Machine-class citizens are permitted to reproduce annually, Bob says. The lottery is run by the station government of each individual station. Each citizen is permitted a single ticket, delivered physically to them on the first day of each year.

When do they decide who gets to have babies? Micah demands. On the last day of the year?

Indeed, Bob says.

So basically every one of these hard-working stiffs has an entire year to misplace, lose or destroy their ticket. How many people actually claim their winnings?

This lottery season, one hundred thirteen citizens claimed their reproductive authorizations, Bob says.

So eighty-seven people, probably through pure, dumb luck, don't get to start a family this year, Micah says.

Your math is correct, sir.

And how many Onyx babies were born last year?

One hundred eleven thousand four hundred seventy one, Bob answers.

Micah turns back to the window. He pinches the bridge of his nose, thinking hard. How many Onyx citizens are there right now? he asks.

Bob says, One million two hundred eighty four thousand six hundred nine.

And how many Machine-class citizens?

Six million three hundred forty seven —

Stop, stop. I get it. You're telling me that the Onyx class is outnumbered by six to one —

That's not entirely accurate —

But it's close enough. They're outnumbered six to one, so they're having as many babies as they can, while the working class advances at a microscopic pace. So in, what — fifteen years? — the Onyx class outnumbers the working class altogether?

That's not entirely accurate, either.

But is that the goal? Of course my math isn't right. This is bullshit.

That is not a stated goal of the program, sir.

Onyx isn't trying to quickly grow so it can't be easily overthrown by a blue-collar riot?

No, sir.

Micah paces around the room. The sun is beginning to rise over the city again.

So what's the goal of this reproductive Nazism?

I don't believe that's an accurate term for it either, sir. But the goal is quite simple. Humanity is attempting to create successive generations of smarter, more creative and more forward-thinking people. After all, did you believe that mankind would simply relocate from Earth to Earth orbit and be satisfied with its future?

Micah stops. What are you saying?

The fleet of stations is just the first step in a very long-term plan, Bob says, to find a new home for humanity. Several, if possible.

But to manipulate the race as you go, right? Like you're breeding show dogs or racehorses.

I'm not responsible, sir. I'm simply an artificial

intelligence, a companion designated to serve you.

Serve? Or observe and report?

Sir, your activities in your apartment are only recorded so that I may provide more nuanced service as I grow more informed about your preferences and requirements, Bob says.

This is bullshit, Micah says again. Bullshit.

I believe that you will find the Onyx-class life a pleasant one, sir. Onyx-class citizens are not required to hold regular positions of employment, but are provided with ample time to spend on whatever personal projects, hobbies or leisures they wish, Bob says. Onyx-class citizens have large amounts of time, and with it, they produce novels, fine artwork, political position papers, beautiful music, complex theorems and more.

But if I wanted to just sleep all day and all night, every day and night? I could do that, couldn't I.

You may spend your time however you wish, Bob says.

What if I wish to spend my time with the Machine class? What if I want to take a job, or visit a friend?

Visitations are permitted and in fact encouraged, Bob says.

But?

But Machine-class employment for Onyx-class citizens is prohibited.

Micah paces again. Mae would never have gone for this.

It is possible that is true, Bob says.

What do you mean?

Mae Atherton-Sparrow, your deceased wife from whom you inherited your Onyx-class status, did not complete the twelve-week course. She successfully completed just under two weeks of the course.

Micah presses his palms against his eyes. And what is the curriculum for those first two weeks?

In order, Bob says, the first two weeks prepare future settlers for low-gravity transport, set packing guidelines, discuss medical waivers, allow selection of living quarters, and teach settlers about the changed day and night patterns.

When are the details of Onyx- and Machine-class policies taught? Micah asks.

On week nine, Bob says.

Week nine, Micah repeats. Mae didn't know about any of this.

It's unlikely, sir.

You know, Micah says, I didn't want to live in space. Mae did. When she died — when she died, I was miserable for seven long, stupid years. And then one day I woke up and realized I'd let nearly a decade pass without doing anything positive. I slept all the time. I worked a shit job, and I considered becoming a drunk. But after those seven years, I suddenly wanted to do something for Mae. It took me seven years, but I wanted to honor her. So I applied for settlement. Imagine my surprise when I was not only accepted, but granted elite status.

Inheritors are truly fortunate people, Bob agrees.

No, Micah says. No. We might just be the only ones who are thinking clearly.

Micah steps out of the shower.

Bob, he says.

Yes, sir.

How exactly does a person dry off around here?

If you'll re-enter the shower, sir, I'll happily demonstrate, Bob says.

Micah opens the shower door and steps back inside.

Bob says, Any time you'd like to dry yourself, simply say the word 'dry'.

Okay, Micah says. Dry.

The shower doors hiss. Previously unseen seals tighten and pop into place. The shower becomes an isolation chamber. Micah thinks nervously about what might happen if the shower activated now. Would the chamber fill with water? Could he drown in an upright shower chamber?

Around him, dozens of tiny specks become visible in the walls. The specks form a grid pattern. Micah is reaching out to touch them when they activate. Each speck is a tiny jet. His skin ripples and rearranges itself in the blast from the miniature blasts. He feels his hair flipping about, and looks up.

Mistake. The jets in the ceiling pound his eyes, which moisten immediately.

Try not to look at the jets, sir, Bob says.

Don't watch me in the shower, Bob, Micah says.

Three tones sound as Bob processes this. Micah imagines Bob as a tiny spook with a notepad.

Does not like it when you watch him in shower. Check.

⤮

*H*ello?

    Mae.

    I thought we agreed not to —

I'm sorry. I miss you. And it's ridiculous, not talking.

It's not ridiculous. Micah, we have a real problem.

Your boss called.

Oh.

He said that a package had arrived for you marked time-sensitive. He wanted to know if he should have somebody messenger it over while you were on sabbatical.

What did you say?

I said that's what he should do.

Good.

Sabbatical?

Look, I don't want to talk about it.

Are you actually in Tokyo, or did you lie about everything?

I'm in Tokyo.

Good. Okay. Why?

I told you, we're not talking right now.

I'm talking. You're not talking.

Micah, I don't need this.

This? I'm just a 'this' to you?

You know you're not.

I have tried being understanding.

You've done a bang-up job at it.

Hey. I have tried.

Micah, tell me one thing.

What?

Tell me what your single biggest dream is.

I don't know.

You know you have one. What is it?

Maybe to live in the house. And I'm doing it, so mission accomplished.

Alright. So what if I had stayed in California?

When?

Instead of moving in with you at the house. What if I had put my foot down? What if I had said you have to move to California with me, or we're through?

I — you wouldn't have.

No, but if I had. Do you know what would have happened? I know you do. We would have broken up, Micah. Because the house is important to you. Because it holds almost an entire lifetime of meaning, and you'll never be shaken free from that. You would never want to. And I understood that, and I would never have tried to change that.

But that's exactly what you want to do now. You want to shake me free of that and take me to Pluto.

Yes, well. I do. But now it's very personal.

Why?

Because now I know that there are limits to how far you'll go to see me happy, Micah. Once you know that, you can't really go back on it.

That's such a harsh way to put it.

But it's true, Micah. It isn't a lie. It might suck to hear, but it's the truth.

Why are you in Tokyo?

It's alright. You can change the subject.

Thanks. Why are you in Tokyo?

I just am.

With somebody?

Of course not.

Because I kind of get the feeling that when you come back, everything ends. And if I have that feeling, maybe you already have that feeling, too. And maybe you figure there's no reason not to act on that feeling.

Do you realize how much we fight now? Do you think I want to come back to that?

Are you seeing somebody?

Oh, fuck you, Micah. Go back to bed.

～◎～

Bob, where do I go if I want to work?

You are not required to work, sir.

Yes, I know that. But surely there are Onyx-class people who do.

Onyx-class citizens create their own jobs.

What if the job I want is not predicting social change, or writing a novel? What if I just want to push a button two thousand times a day? Or carry food to people? What if I want to run a machine press?

Bob says, You will not be permitted to have any of those jobs. Those jobs are reserved for Machine-class citizens.

Okay, what if I want to be a Machine-class citizen? Micah asks.

You can't switch your class, unfortunately, Bob answers.

No? What about Machine-class people? Can they ever become Onyx-class citizens?

Bob pauses. There are certain exceptions to the standard rule that allow for that possibility.

Oh? And what are these exceptions?

If you were to wed a Machine-class citizen, they would inherit your status as your partner, and retain your status after your death, Bob says.

That's interesting. I'm surprised that would be allowed.

Marriage of a Machine-class citizen is only permitted if the Machine-class citizen is female and expecting the child of an Onyx-class citizen, Bob clarifies.

Micah shrugs into his jacket. That's perverse, he says.

Intimate relationships between Onyx-class and Machine-class citizens require approval from Station Administration.

Micah gapes. The government permits or denies — what the —

As I mentioned before, sir, Bob says, the Onyx program is a social experiment.

Are all twelve stations structured this way?

The Onyx program is still in its pilot phase, Bob says. Station Argus is its proving ground.

So if there were, say, a Machine-class riot that overthrew the Onyx-class rule, this insane system wouldn't be adopted for the other eleven stations?

I suppose that's accurate, Bob says.

Huh, Micah says.

Bob says, There are protections in place to prevent such an uprising.

I'm sure. Bob, Micah says, tell me where I can get some food.

～☺～

Micah leaves the apartment and rides the lift tube to the top of the petal, four hundred fifteen floors above his own. The tube is transparent and runs along a central rail of the inner petal, providing a breathtaking view of Station Argus, fully unfolded. He is transfixed by the city below, more vast than any he has ever seen. Its towers and curving transport lines turn golden in the sun's glare. From so high, the travel pods look like dewdrops on the tendril of a plant.

Micah had watched an animation on Earth that demonstrated the station's flower-like properties. The station had no stem, but its central city was flanked by ten massive petals shaped like sails. The city itself was constructed on an immense retractable platform.

On days of particularly disruptive or dangerous solar flares, or if a stray asteroid ventured too close, the giant city would retract deep into the belly of the station, and the ten petals would turn and fold inward, locking together to transform Station Argus into a floating canister. Completely sealed, the station was as impenetrable as an oyster.

He shakes his head. If he'd known about the class system —

Would he still have come?

How else would he have honored Mae's memory?

Maybe another station.

But he knows that Argus is the only station currently accepting new settlers. It is the newest of the fleet, and has not yet reached its population control level.

All he had wanted was to carve out a small life, one as small as his had been on Earth, and to wake up each morning to watch the sunrise, and to have a cup of coffee and remember his wife. This new reality seems contrary to his simple goal. After just one brief conversation with Bob, Micah feels like a conspirator on the wrong side of a great and inhumane battle.

The lift carries him to the top of the petal — at least as high as residents are permitted to visit. The observation deck — and to his horror, restaurant and nightclub — are still several hundred feet from the top of the tower.

A woman in a crisp dark suit meets him as he exits the lift.

Good day, sir, she says.

Hi, he says.

Seating for one? she asks.

Um, Micah says. Actually, I was just hoping to take a look from the top. If I can do that.

Of course, the woman says. You're free to move about as you choose, of course.

He nods at her as he passes, wondering if she's Machine-class. He can't imagine that the station permits Onyx-class citizens to work in the food service industry, so she must be. Is she married? Is she hoping this year for a child? What sort of work does her husband do?

Is she happy?

Micah glances back at her. She has moved back to a small, transparent podium, and is standing quite still, watching the lift indicators closely.

He feels for her. What a life.

Get it together, he thinks. *You're projecting your own feelings onto her right now. She's probably perfectly happy. She gets to live in space! No glow-in-the-dark stars pasted to the ceiling of her bedroom at night — she gets the real thing! Where do you get off?*

The hostess turns then and smiles at him.

Get moving, Micah.

He does.

◦◦◦

The observation platform is glorious, and terrifying. Micah is not the only person here. Several other people have already braved their fears and were floating above the city. Some are nearby, ready to return to the tower quickly if needed. Others, perhaps more daring, are quite distant and small.

Behind him is an alcove in the outer wall of the tower. This closet is filled with personal body jets, and Micah watches as a young man helps another into the suit. In fact, suit is the last word for the body jets. Rather, the attire is a simple exoskeleton that the wearer fits over his arms, legs, shoulders and spine. At pivot points, tiny attitude jets jut from the frame.

Excuse me, says the young man.

Micah steps back and watches as the man and his friend venture to the red line. An imprint on the floor reads:

PERSONAL GRAVITY DISABLED PAST THIS POINT

DO NOT PROCEED WITHOUT BODY JET OR TETHER

The two men walk to the red line.

Ready? the first man says.

The second man looks dubious, but he nods.

It's easy, says the first, stepping over the line.

As soon as he crosses the line, his body stops being defined by his feet. He becomes lighter, and drifts very slowly upward, following the momentum of his final footsteps. He moves his hands a bit, and Micah sees the tiny jets fire imperceptibly from his shoulders, bringing him to an almost certain halt.

The second man joins him, and after a few moments of reorienting himself, the two fire their bodyjets and sail out over the city. Micah watches them with a sense of wonder. From there, they must be able to see everything. Argus City's tallest spires are not so far below. Maybe they can even see people in the buildings.

It occurs to him then to wonder about the buildings themselves. If the million or so Onyx-class citizens don't commute to jobs there, then do only Machine-class people work there? Why would Onyx citizens need to visit the city at all? What purpose does it serve?

Again, he feels suffused with a sense of imbalance. He looks out over the station. Pale and hazy in the distance, he can see the farthest of the Onyx petals. He sees the station differently now, as though the Onyx-class citizens are on a shining hillside, looking down upon the peasants in the village.

He watches the floating people in bodyjets. They're pointing and looking below.

As if the city is a zoo, and they themselves are free.

*W*hen are you coming home?

    I don't know, Micah. It's nice here, and I like it.

What are you doing with yourself?

I tour the city. I eat good food.

Are you happy?

I'm enjoying myself. But I don't know if I'm happy.

I'm not happy.

You linger over all of the things I do here. I keep wondering about us. It's turning into a scab that I can't stop scratching at.

Now I'm a scab?

You know what I mean. It's like an itch I can't scratch. Until we figure things out, it's going to be a distraction.

A distraction.

You know what I mean. Stop that.

What's that sound? Are you at a party?

I'm on a train, actually. People talk on trains.

Why are you on a train? I heard that trains in Japan are dangerous.

Not for a long time, Micah. But thank you for worrying about me. It's nice to know that you still think I can't take care of myself.

That's not what I meant, Mae.

I'm on the train back to Tokyo. I went to Kyoto for the day.

Kyoto is Tokyo rearranged.

Yeah, I hadn't thought of that before. That's nice.

You went for the day?

Yeah.

Isn't it far?

It's only an hour.

Fast train.

Yeah. Micah, I want to enjoy the view, okay. Can we talk later?

Are you coming home?

Not for a little while. There's something here I'm doing.

What are you doing?

It's nothing. I'll tell you about it another time.

I don't like this. I miss you.

We'll talk later.

Mae? I miss you.

I believe you, Micah. I'm sure you mean it.

I do.

Okay. I believe you. I'm going to go now.

Do you miss me?

Goodbye, Micah.

MAE

His last words to her made him feel ashamed. Desperate.

Do you miss me?

He didn't like the person he was then. For seven years after, he buried himself in his grief. When he was tempted to examine himself, he resisted. He learned to pretend that he wasn't really there. What he did with himself didn't matter. He gained weight, and didn't care. He went to work and home again in a haze, and didn't care. He slept often, woke up, and slept more.

One night he saw an infomercial for a neural product called the Dreambake. He didn't like the name, in fact had visions of the product actually overheating his skull until his brain became a fluffy pastry. He had never purchased anything that he had seen in an informercial before, but this time he considered it. The Dreambake was supposed to allow you to influence your dreams. It came with a manual input, allowing you to specify with startling precision the details of the dream you wanted to have, but it also had a learning feature. It would extrapolate from brain activity the deepest passions that lay dormant within your psyche, and then activate them once you slept.

He worked his shit job with Todd, a sallow-faced young man who probably only left his house to work. Todd saved his money for six months, and bought the Dreambake. With his disposable income he stocked up on sleep aids.

I literally sleep from the moment I get home from work until the moment I have to get ready for my next shift, he said to Micah one day.

Why? Micah had asked.

Because that way I can dream more, Todd confessed. It's overwhelming and it's awesome.

What do you dream about?

Different things. Sometimes I go all-in for the big spy-movie fantasies, you know. I'm running around with great clothes and hair, and I have to take out an informant before he sells his secrets to the other guy.

Todd leaned closer.

Micah leaned away.

Mostly, though, Todd had said, I dream about Erika.

Who is Erika? Micah asked.

Erika! Todd said, smacking Micah on the shoulder. Come on, man. You haven't noticed? She runs the checkout up front? Kind of girl who should be some rich asshole's trophy, not selling groceries. Erika. You know?

Micah vaguely knew who Todd was talking about. Erika, he had said.

Right. Erika! And man, let me tell you, Todd said. Let me tell you. She wouldn't talk to me at all. Said good morning to her once, and when she noticed it was me she just kept walking. It's alright, I don't blame her. I mean, look at me, Mikey.

Micah, Micah said.

Look at me. See? You get it. I get it. Hell, everybody gets it. But man, when I go home? I uploaded a photo of her into my Dreambake, see. And now she does whatever I want in my dreams.

Micah had perked up. Yeah?

See, I knew you'd come around. Best eighteen thousand dollars I ever spent. Yeah, man. Anything I want.

What if —

Naw, man. Ask. Go on. It's awesome. I don't mind telling.

What if you just wanted her to be herself? Micah

had asked.

Be herself? Todd roared. Man, herself shuts me down like I'm nobody to her. Which, you know. I am. So fuck that, man. In my dream, she thinks I'm the shit. Besides, it ain't like the Dreambake knows anything about her. It just recreates her from the photo I gave it.

Could it, though? I mean, if you could tell the —

The Dreambake.

— the Dreambake about her, could it make her actually behave like her real self?

Todd shrugs. I don't know, man. It's not like this is future tech. It is what it is. I think you pretty much have to tell it everything you want it to do, and then it does it.

Huh, Micah had said.

Man, let me tell you what she did last night, Todd went on.

Micah waved him off. No, that's alright. Please don't.

You sure?

Sure, Micah had said.

That night he had replayed the infomercial twenty times. He studied the product carefully, but nowhere among the many conversations about it online could he find the answer to his question. He posted on a forum and explained his problem, and he was swamped by messages of sympathy from strangers. But nobody could answer his question.

It wasn't a difficult question.

Will the Dreambake help me talk to my wife one last time?

He wasn't stupid. He knew it wouldn't count for anything — that Mae was gone, and no matter what he might say to a tech toy, that would never change.

But he thought that it might make him feel a little better.

Shake him out of this nearly decade-long depression he was courting.

Eighteen thousand dollars wasn't a problem. He spent almost none of his income. He worked to forget her. His wages fell into his bank account without fanfare, day after day. He had nearly three hundred thousand dollars there, saved from years of unpacking boxes and stocking shelves.

Eighteen thousand dollars was nothing.

Hell, it cost less than eighteen thousand dollars to go to space these days.

Micah had sat up in bed at the thought.

In the morning, he resigned his position at the market.

The next afternoon, he was holding Mae's Onyx card.

~◦~

I *guess I can't really stop you from calling, can I.*

Well, you don't have to answer.

Yes, but when it says Micah, I sort of feel like I should. I feel like it's chastising me when I don't.

Jesus, Mae. How did we end up here so fast?

I don't know. It was pretty fast, wasn't it.

I just want you to come home.

I —

Or I'll come to you. Let me come to you.

Micah, I don't know. Something doesn't feel right anymore.

Is it really just the space thing, Mae? Is there more to it?

If you're asking me that, then I think you've missed the real point, Micah.

Come home, Mae. We can work it out. I miss you.

I — Micah, I miss you, too.

Really? Oh, this is like music. I can book a flight.

But I'm not coming home.

Mae...

I said before, I have something to do here.

What is it? Tell me what it is. I won't be upset.

Micah, I can't.

I promise. I won't be.

Okay. Promise?

I swear.

There's someone else, Micah.

⤳ଡ଼౿

He hated those dreams.

They always carried a promise of hope, sang it to him as he slept. In his dreams, Mae was hesitant, still gun-shy, but crumbling. He was gallant, willing to set aside all of his flaws, willing to consider almost anything if it meant they could be happy again.

And then the dreams took awful, terrible turns.

In them, Mae was having affairs. Sometimes just one, but in the heightened horror of Micah's dream-state, often many, simultaneously. Sometimes they were one-night stands, a quick fuck in some stranger's apartment, or worse, on the Tokyo train. Micah had heard of these things. His dreams capitalized on his fears.

But none of these things were real, and Mae didn't feel an obligation in the real world to answer his calls anymore. They went unanswered, his pleading messages unreturned.

Perhaps she was preparing him for the end, he wonders now.

If she was, she did a piss-poor job of it.

~∾~

He had just come back from town.

The beach house was hazy in the fog, mostly hidden from view. He could hear the water, but couldn't see it. It was calm, almost still.

He closed the door of his Jeep, crunched across the pebbled driveway to the front door.

Mae wasn't home, of course. He missed coming home to a house that was drenched in shadow, except for the single light beside her reading chair. She wouldn't turn on more lights than she was actively using, even though the climate crisis was decades behind them and the damage long since done.

The house was empty.

He'd left the lights on.

His wrist hummed, and he looked down at the display to see a missed call. He must not have felt the tickle of an incoming call. Maybe it came while he was turning into the bumpy driveway.

He tapped the display, and in his ear, the worst message of his life unspooled, spoken by an eerily calm Japanese voice, and cross-translated by his ear tab. The message was brief — was he the husband of Mae Atherton-Sparrow, the American space station trainee? If so, would he please return this call?

And he knew.

In the dark of his grandfather's beach house, the one he had hoped to raise children in, the one he hoped to grow very old in, the one he had so proudly introduced Mae too, the one that he had constructed his dreams around since he was a child, he knew.

～◎～

Micah wakes before the first sunrise of the morning, which is scheduled to happen at 4:32 a.m. It occurs to him that, 33,000 miles above his home, his sense of time has vanished. He wonders if Station Argus is high enough above the Earth to have affected the way time works. Yes, he imagines. But he decides that nobody has rewritten the number of minutes in the day for purely nostalgic reasons.

Knowing that twenty-four/seven hasn't changed is one of the most basic comforts, he imagines, for those who have chosen to step off of the spinning ball they were raised on.

Bob says, Good morning, sir.

Micah doesn't respond. He's only sleeping in his apartment, in this bed, because he doesn't know how to access his finances. He feels strangely like a traitor, though he cannot decide whom he has betrayed. He settles on Bernard, and Mae. By accepting this privileged existence, by leaning on it, he feels as if he is being disrespectful to that kind old man and his granddaughter, and as if he is thumbing his nose at the memory of his deceased wife, who was the sweetest of souls.

If he knew how to get to his money, he'd have stayed in a hotel in Argus City last night.

He'd have looked for a place of his own.

May I recommend a breakfast selection, sir? Perhaps a coffee?

No, thank you, Micah says. Let's continue with the education selection of your programming. Tell me where I can find my bank account. And how do I shop for food?

Sir, your assets were neutralized upon entry into the Onyx system, Bob says.

Micah wishes that Bob had a face so that he could stare dumbfounded at it. I worked for most of my

life to save that money, he says, finally. And it was —
neutralized?

Onyx-class citizens enjoy unfettered access to all
station systems, sir, Bob says. You will have no need
for funds. To order food, simply speak your list of
items, and it will be delivered to your apartment in
as timely a manner as you wish. All other services are
similarly free of charge.

Free, Micah repeats. I get everything for free.

Yes, sir, Bob says.

Such as?

Bob says, There are no charges or fees for your
apartment or its support systems. Food is free of
charge. Entertainment of all types, including physical,
is free of charge. Clothing and any items you wish
to purchase, including customizations for your
apartment, are free of charge. Body modifications and
enhancements, including neural adjustments, are free
of charge.

Physical entertainment?

Physical entertainment is a polite way to describe
intimate companionship, Bob explains.

Whores, then.

That is a less-polite way to describe it, sir, but you
are correct.

Who chooses to be a prostitute in space? Micah
wonders aloud.

Physical companionship is one of the four
thousand seven hundred sixteen employment channels
that Machine-class citizens are preselected for, Bob

says.

Preselected, Micah repeats. You mean, the government taps new arrivals and says, You're a ship mechanic, you're a bartender, you're a gardener, you're a... piece of meat?

Machine-class citizens are invited to submit their qualifications for their preferred positions, Bob says. Physical companions often select that line of employment for themselves. I believe the consensus is that it is less physically-taxing than other Machine-class employment positions, and therefore, in some segments of the population, a desired position. Like other more interesting employment positions, physical companionship is one option with a waiting list.

Micah shakes his head. Okay, I can't think about that anymore.

As you wish, sir.

So the things that are free to me, Micah says. Are those only things I can get in the tower here?

No, sir, Bob says. Services that are free to you can be found all over Station Argus, both in the towers and in Argus City.

So I could go to the city today and buy a sandwich.

Of course, sir. At no cost to you.

I could buy a new wardrobe.

Yes, sir. At no cost.

I could visit the holopark.

Yes, sir, Bob repeats. At no cost.

I could... stay in a hotel?

In theory, sir. I would be remiss not to instruct you

that sleeping out-of-quarters will raise an alert that you did not return to your apartment.

An alert. You mean someone tracks me.

I track you, sir, Bob says.

Stop tracking me, Bob.

I'm not at liberty to do so, sir. Personal tracking is less invasive than you may think. I simply observe your activities in order to better serve you.

So if I didn't come home —

In that case, sir, I am required to submit an alert to station government.

You have to tell *the government* if I don't come home at night? Jesus.

I am required to inform the station government, sir, and when you return to your apartment, you would be contacted by an administrator. The administrator would be charged with ascertaining why you did not return to your quarters at night.

Jesus fuck, Micah says. Why is that anybody's business but my own?

Absence from your apartment can be an indicator of several scenarios that the government must monitor, sir, Bob says. For example, it may indicate that you have begun a physical relationship with a Machine-class citizen.

Which is the government's business *why*?

Such a relationship may lead to complexities regarding that Machine-class citizen's status. If that citizen were impregnated, for example, without administration approval —

Holy shit, Micah says. I don't want to hear this.

— then protocol regarding said pregnancy would go into effect.

You're talking about abortion. You're talking about forced government-sponsored abortion. Population control.

No, sir. Not strictly population control. Unauthorized class expansion is taken quite seriously. As I mentioned before, Onyx-class citizens are welcomed and even encouraged to reproduce among themselves as frequently as they like.

This is one goddamn horrible experiment you're running on this station, Bob.

I am simply your apartment's artificial intelligence, sir.

We'll see about that, Micah said.

He pulled on his clothes, threw open the door, and stomped into the hallway, still pulling on his coat.

Bob closed the door behind him.

⚬⚬

What did you think when you first saw me?

We've talked about this before, haven't we?

Tell me again.

Well, I thought there was no one more beautiful in the whole world.

And you wanted to marry me right then and there.

I wanted to marry you a thousand times in one day.

And you wanted lots of babies.

All of the babies.

Did you think, wow, check out that bod.

I didn't.

Not even a little bit? I'm sad.

I really didn't. I was captivated just watching you smile and laugh.

You didn't even notice my butt? I have a very nice butt.

You were standing behind that food cart. I couldn't see your butt.

Ah, so you tried.

I didn't. But I'm sure if I had seen your butt, I really would have liked it.

You're a pervert.

I remember thinking, I bet she looks this amazing in any light. Because it was a very lovely morning, and the sun was shining through your hair and doing that thing where it makes you almost glow. And I thought, you probably glow at night, in the dark.

Like a radioactive princess.

My radioactive princess.

Micah.

Yes.

I'm sorry.

Sorry? What for?

For all of this. Look around. It's not what I wanted.

It's kind of scary, isn't it.

I wanted to have babies in in space, in the glow of a star, to make them shine and then push them out into the dark and let them light up the universe.

You're such a romantic.

I wanted to huddle together with you over a space campfire, all of the darkness around us, and know that we were special, we were together, we were the only two people for a hundred million trillion miles.

And instead, it's terrifying.

I don't even feel like I know who human beings are anymore.

They say it's an experiment, Mae.

It's a horrible one. You thought that the lower-class citizens were like animals in a zoo, but you were wrong. You all are.

The thought occurred to me.

What are you going to do?

I don't know. I could start a revolution.

I bet a lot of people have tried that.

You think?

It's scary how much they know about you already.

They probably know I'm not feeling their little utopia, I guess.

Not feeling it at all.

In fact, they're probably watching me right now.

Watching you sleep? Probably.

Is that what I'm doing? Sleeping?

You thought there was another way we could be talking?

I didn't buy the Dreambake.

Good. Infomercial products are garbage. It probably would kill all of your brain cells at one time.

But this is the conversation that I would have dreamed of if I had.

Maybe.

Maybe?

You weren't living in an oppressive cage at the time.

You could argue that my grief was a cage.

Yes, but you made that cage.

I was oppressing myself.

You were sad, Micah.

I was sad.

I know. If it had been different, I would have been sad, too.

I couldn't believe that you were gone. And that I wasn't with you when it happened.

I'm sorry.

I'm sorry, too.

What are you going to do now, Micah?

Probably not start a revolution. I don't think I'd be very good at it.

You could marry again. Have space babies.

I can't even think about that. I don't look at women like that. Nobody is you.

They don't have to be me. They just have to make you happy.

They don't.

What does?

I don't know. The beach house didn't even work after you died.

You haven't been happy in seven years?

Seven years and one terrible argument.

That's awful, Micah. It's my fault.

It's mine, too.

So we're both responsible for your life being tragic.

Yes, I guess so.

Chivalrous of you to take all of the responsibility.
Hey, you did kind of run away to Tokyo.
I did. So I guess you're right, it's kind of my fault, too.
I'll settle for that.
So. What will you do?

༺❀༻

A rgus City dazzles in the darkness.
Constellations of light, the flicker of pods darting between the spires. Sparkling towers constructed from seamless transparent steel catch the moonlight and throw it around like fine china that splinters and turns.

Micah is alone tonight.

It's not even night. It's two in the afternoon, but the sun has dropped behind the Earth, and only the faintest golden glow breaks the planet's crisp horizon line.

If he closes his eyes, can almost convince himself that he's still on Earth. His ears reproduce the soft, papery surge of the waves. He can feel the damp wood planks of the pier beneath his feet. He remembers the most important voices that he ever heard in exactly that spot. His grandfather's, telling him that one day they would build a boat together, and that if it sank, then they would build a ship in a bottle instead.

And Mae's, closer, her breath on his neck, simply saying good morning.

Mae.

Mae.

Micah fits his arms into the bodyjet, and steps back, clicking his feet into the heel clips. The exoskeleton feels kind of nice against his limbs. A cradle for his fragile human body, perhaps.

What does one say in a moment such as this one? He settles for nothing at all.

~⊚~

What did you think? When you first saw me?

 That you were the most handsome man I had ever seen.

Bullshit. You didn't think that at all.

You're right.

Am I? Damn. I don't like being right.

You're right. I didn't think anything, because you put my brain into a coma.

That was pretty mean of me.

Oh, I don't know. It's been a fine coma-dream.

The finest, Mae.

I miss you.

I love you.

~⊚~

Micah steps across the red line.

 He hangs there, suspended, just a couple of feet from the safety and artificial gravity of the observation deck.

I could go back, he thinks.

He looks down. The great petal narrows as it falls away beneath him. Hundreds of windows, some of them dimmed, most glowing with activity. He wonders if anybody is looking outside, looking up. Does anybody see him up here?

The city swims away beneath him, bursting with activity.

The zoo.

He glances back at the observation deck and is startled to see a face in the window. It belongs to the hostess from a few days ago. He meets her gaze, and she lifts a hand. He offers a smile.

She looks upward, at the blackness beyond the ring of petals.

He follows her gaze. The ten towers, like points of a crown. The doorway to beyond that exists between them.

The hostess smiles back, and waves once more. Then she turns from the window and is gone.

Mae, Micah thinks.

He fires the tiny attitude jets, turning his back to the tower.

The sun is beginning to rise.

He turns his face into its warmth, fires the jets, and rises with it.

Argus City recedes.

Micah approaches, and then passes the ring of petals.

The sun is warm, but everything else is so cold.

Mae.

THE LAST
RAIL-RIDER

The first time I stole away on a boxcar, I was hooked.

There was so much to love about the rails that I felt my heart might explode. The damp smell of the wood, the tang of oil. The faint whiff of ancient strawberries on the night breeze as the train chugged and swayed through dead farmland and withered orchards. Some cars had roof hatches, and short ladders, and if you were careful, you could lie on your back and feel the train beneath you like a horse, the toxic pomegranate-colored sky rocking overhead.

But my favorite part was the secrets. I didn't know that there were other rail-riders like me, but there must have been. Long ago, perhaps. I certainly hadn't seen anyone else in the shadows, or curled up in hay bales in a musty car. I found my first hint at the riders of the world gone by after I'd been riding the rails for a few months. I'd camped out in a car that had once been painted red, but was now the color of dried blood, flaky and worn. The floor was chewed away, and there were gaps in the wall planks, and the roof sagged and bounced with every jostle of the tracks. I was afraid for a little while that it would collapse on me in my sleep, and then I decided that if it was going to, it would have done so long before I found my way into this car, and this logic put my mind at ease.

There was a burlap sack in the corner, gnawed through by rodents or bugs, and I pulled it over myself for warmth. It was rough and scratchy, and that was something else to like about being a rail-rider. You ran into things. You felt them in a way other people didn't. It was probable that nobody else on the whole of the earth knew what that sack felt like up close, but I did.

I slept for a time, the train like a gentle sea bearing me into the dark, the hustle and groan of the old cars stitching a comfortable blanket of white noise for me to sink into. When I woke, it was morning, and the red sun streamed through the seams in the walls like playground slides made of pure light. The train had stopped. I peeked between two planks at the land outside the car, expecting to see a rail station. Instead, I saw old cattle fields, long abandoned, the churned-up black soil of the yards gone gray and dry in the sun, weeds crawling up where they once would have been chewed or beaten back into the earth by a thousand stupid hooves.

This wasn't a planned stop. Which meant I needed

to get moving.

I grabbed the sack — it had served me well, and I thought it should come with me — and rolled it tightly. But there was something inside, blocky and hard. I hadn't noticed it during the night, and there was no time to investigate now. I could hear the crunch of footsteps on the cinder track bed outside. I crawled to the largest hole in the floor and dropped through, landing on the cinders as the heavy plank door grated open above me.

∿◉◠

Rail security checks were the worst. I knew that they hadn't seen me climb aboard. I rode a different line every day if I could, or every couple of days at least, but every last one had a man or two who spot-checked the boxcars at unexpected intervals. I'd never been caught, but one day I would be, and I didn't know what they did to stowaways like me.

Like me.

That was my other clue. It didn't make sense that all these different security men would be looking for me, which meant that they had to be looking for people like me. Which suggested that I wasn't the first, nor the only.

I slept in a dried-out cornfield that night, wading a few feet deep into the headless stalks, and bedding down between them, careful not to lean on them. Someone might see a strange gap in the ceiling above me if I did, and I didn't know if other folks were anything like the railway men, but I erred on the side of caution. I tended to believe that nobody anywhere would be happy to see me, ever, and that usually served me well. I stayed out of sight, and so far, I was still in one piece. I'd seen people who weren't.

I unfolded the burlap sack, and remembered the strange lump I'd felt in it. I shook out the bag, and a tidy little book, tied up with a leather strip, tumbled out onto the dusty ground. I stared at it, not sure what to think, or even if I was thinking at all. It was smaller than a brick. The cover was dark brown, and looked like it might once have been part of a rubber boot. It was scuffed on the outside, and when I unwound the string and opened the cover, I saw a fibrous, fabric texture on the inside. Exactly like a rain boot.

The pages didn't match, and some of them had things printed on them that didn't belong. Some of the pages were cloth and some were paper, all cobbled and gathered together from different raw materials. There was the rough crinkled texture of a flour sack, and a stiff piece of corrugated cardboard, and maybe part of a shoebox, and a manila folder. And every last page was scribbled on, its available spaces crammed with tight, small writing.

I couldn't read any of it. None of it was any language I'd ever seen, and my English comprehension was pretty rough around the edges to begin with. Some of the writing looked like symbols, and some of the pictures I thought I recognized. One looked like bread. One looked like a campfire.

It got dark, and I put the book aside and stretched out my legs, feeling the dull ache of a long day in my knees and ankles. I slept, but only for an hour or so, because in the dark I heard the quiet metal crawl of another train.

∽⊚∾

The way I heard it was that there weren't many towns any more because they'd all caved in from emptiness.

I heard that some of them sank, and some of them got burned up, and some of them just blew up. I was born after the skies turned black, so I don't really re-member what the towns were like before. Someone told me once that there were eleven billion people out there, just walking around, taking up space. Eleven billion. I thought ten people was a lot. That was more people than I'd seen in months. I couldn't put my head around eleven billion.

There weren't that many people any more.

The skies weren't so black these days, either. The sun was a red ember behind red clouds. The sky wasn't blue, like I'd heard it once was, but red seemed like it might be better than black. It burned down hot and dry, and sometimes, as the trains carved through the old valleys, you could see some old forgotten house, out in the middle of nothing and nowhere, just burning up, spitting sparks and oily smoke at the clouds.

I caught the night train and rode for a long, long time. I hadn't seen this part of the country before. I sat on the edge of the car with my feet dangling out, and I ate some stale peanuts and watched the hills rise and fall. Everything was dead, like everywhere else, but this stretch of track looked different. Better somehow.

But it wasn't.

＊

The trains were the only thing still moving out here. There were other old vehicles, rusted out and melted into crumbling blacktop, but I'd never seen one that wasn't rusted or bombed-out. I never saw anyone on the roads, or crossing the black fields. I used to, but it might have been years since that was common. Used to be you could look out there and see little knots of people, tiny and disoriented, like survivors of the worst kind of tragedy, just aimlessly trudging along the horizon. Now if you looked hard, you might see still lumps on the distant meadows. Bodies, just worn out, given up.

Sometimes I thought that the railway men and I were the only folks left in all the world. That was reassuring, somehow. I felt a bit like a survivor, like I'd won something I hadn't counted on winning. The trains were alive, and so was I, and almost nobody else was. I felt bad, a little, that I'd done this by accident. Like I'd fallen asleep just out of reach of the floods, and awakened to discover that everyone else had drowned.

Once I was chased off a train, and another didn't come along for weeks, and I didn't feel that lucky. I'd found a town called Minnaret, one of the dead towns like every other dead town, and I walked through it, looking around for something to put in my bag. It was well-preserved, mostly, only some of its buildings knocked over. The town smelled bad, though. Like a fart, like rotten eggs. I came around a corner and saw the Minnaret courthouse sticking up out of the ground, still mostly in one piece, just resting in a sinkhole that had opened up. The sides of the hole were stained yellow, and a pale white smoke limply rose from the hole. A sulfur pit. I'd never seen one.

I walked for a while, and I thought about going into one of the houses. I'd never been in a house, not that I could remember. They were supposed to be warm places, I knew, but none of those houses looked warm. They looked like skulls, with dark sockets for windows, with old memories rattling around in their brain pans. Some you could look inside and see old dead bodies, desiccated and tired. I saw one of them slumped over on a porch swing that still creaked in the breeze. So I didn't go into any of the houses.

Instead I went into a supermarket. The windows were all still intact, and there were faded, hand-painted butcher paper signs inside each of them that had cheerful letters and numbers on them. I could read one or two — Soda, 99 cents. Frozen dinners. Sale. The doors were closed and the inside of the store was dark, but I pushed on the door anyway, and it opened, so I went inside. I propped the door open with a shopping cart, then went to all of the windows and pulled down the signs, just for a little bit of light.

The shelves were almost all empty. The store had

been mostly cleaned out, but by a rather polite crowd. Usually you saw a place like this and the windows were all busted, and the shelves were all on their sides, and there was debris and sometimes blood everywhere. But not here. I found an empty cart and pushed it around the store, and anything that I found on the shelves I put into my cart. A jar of pickled onions. A stale loaf of bread in a plastic sleeve.

There was a girl sitting on the floor on the next aisle I came to. I thought at first that she was dead, but then she tilted her head at me, and I lifted my hand and waved. At that time I'd just seen a person a few days before, so I wasn't too scared.

"Hi," I said to her.

She said hello back to me, and I asked her if I could help her up. She just put her arms up like a child. I left my cart and went to her, and took her hands and pulled. Her knees made a terrible cracking sound, so I asked how long she'd been sitting there.

"I don't know."

"Wasn't it dark?"

"Dark everywhere," she said.

She didn't seem interested in talking much after that, and I stood there looking at her, and then she just sat back down in a rush. She didn't look up at me, and I stood there a little longer. And then I went back to my cart and kept pushing, one loose wheel flipping this way and that. Then I left the cart and everything in it, and walked back outside.

Hers was the last voice that I heard.

Until the train I was on stopped in Black Hole, Kentucky.

⤮

I had never heard of Kentucky. I sounded the name out the way I'd sort of learned, once. I knew the words black and hole well enough. The train had stopped abruptly, brakes singing a terrible song, and I heard a muffled popping sound that I'd never heard before. The car I was riding in came to a jerking halt right next to a tin sign printed with the town's name and population, which had once been a little over four thousand people.

I leaned out of the car and looked past the sign. I could see the town clearly enough, just past a wide field of dark soil. It looked less like an intentional town than it did a collection of buildings that happened to be near each other. The town looked like an accident, but a pleasant one. The houses that I could see were colorful and bright, painted in pastel shades that I had never seen before. They were perfectly level and intact. Not a single building looked damaged. I saw chimneys puffing blue smoke and I followed it with my eyes as it curled up into the sky, and then I saw a river of noxious black smoke directly over my head.

I looked up the line. The train engine was engulfed in that same black smoke, and deep inside that smoke I could see flickering orange light. As I watched, a man leaped out of the engine and tumbled down the gravel embankment beside the train. He got to his feet and ran, shouting something I couldn't hear, but the other railway men apparently could, because a moment later seven or eight of them ran down the slope after him. They fled into the field, which was mushy and soft and rich with soil so black it was like the townspeople of Black Hole had been pouring their old cooking grease into the field for years.

Another railway man jumped off of the train, and as I watched, he landed poorly and pitched down the hill head-first. He hit the ground hard and lay still, and when the first group of men saw this, they turned and ran towards the train again. None of them had an easy time of it. They slogged through the soft dirt as if it were swallowing them from beneath. Together, they lifted the injured man by his arms and legs, his head left to dangle at a peculiar angle, and they began to trot as quickly as they could, moving away from the train and back into the grease field.

This concerned me. I didn't want to give myself away, so I decided to stay on the train. Whatever was happening at the front of the train couldn't bother me back here. There must have been forty cars between the engine and my own.

Then the engine blew up.

My boxcar bucked into the air, and the forward wall turned into splinters as the empty freight car ahead of mine punched through it. I jumped out of the car — fell out — and went down the gravel incline like the last of the railway men, at every wrong angle and none of the right ones. I was lucky enough to land flat on my back, and without breaking anything.

A warped hunk of shrapnel sizzled through the red sky and thudded into the earth beside me, hissing and steaming.

A railroad spike.

⌁

Like everything else that afternoon, I was sucked into Black Hole, Kentucky.

Despite the apocalypse happening around me, I didn't particularly want to reveal myself to the railway men, so I ran away from the grease field, away from the engine car. The train was floating on a balloon of fire behind me. I came upon a white clapboard church with a perfect steeple, and I ducked behind it and covered my ears.

A storm of noise and heat bombarded the building at my back, but it died away, and I counted to a thousand before I peeked around the corner.

The train was destroyed. The engine was a twisted bloom of metal and flame, smoke rising up like a dozen black-gloved fists. The rest of the cars had broken free and were scattered around like shattered dinnerware. Flaming bits of wood and oily metal dotted the tracks and the land around it. The tracks themselves were ruined, bent and slung about like shoelaces.

I remembered the book and my burlap sack and the few peanuts that had been left. Everything that I owned in the world, other than my clothes, was gone. I wasn't sad about the peanuts, but I had hoped to figure out more about the book. I had decided that it was a logbook, or perhaps a code manual, for old train-hoppers just like me. Now I would never know for sure.

And I would miss the burlap sack. I had come to like it.

Several of the boxcars and two freight cars had been thrown clear of the tracks, and had landed in the grease field.

They were sinking.

I wasn't the only one to notice. One of the railway men had gone out into the field again, and he was standing atop one of the cars, staring at the carnage around him, shaking his head. The man turned and yelled at his coworkers, who stood at the edge of the field farthest from the tracks, and then he pointed at the car beneath him.

Yep. Definitely sinking. Slowly, but the grease field was dragging the entire boxcar down.

"I've never seen you," a voice behind me said.

I almost jumped out of my shirt. I turned around, afraid I might see a railway man there. But instead I saw a small woman in a tidy green suit and a brown skirt.

She wore a stylish felt hat with flowers in the brim. They looked fresh.

"They're real," she said. "The flowers."

I didn't know what to say, or how to say it.

"You want to know where I got them," she said. "I grow them."

She seemed comfortable with my silence. She looked me up and down with a nod, then said, "You were on the train."

"Don't tell anyone," I said.

"Ah," she answered. "A stowaway. Well, don't let those other fellows see you."

I shook my head. "No, ma'am."

She narrowed her eyes at me, and then she smiled and they flew open wide.

"Come to my house," she exclaimed. "I'll make you some lunch."

"Your house?" I asked.

Her house was nothing like the others. It sat square in the center of a few acres of freshly-cut, bright green grass. A trim white fence held it all in place. The house was painted bright blue, accented by trellises covered with ivy. She opened the gate and led me up a cobblestone path. I could smell cinnamon and apples. I recognized the smell of cinnamon from the supermarket. One of the last items on the shelves had been a small yellow container full of it.

I had sniffed it, and because it smelled nice, I tasted it. It wasn't quite the same.

"I'll make some tea," she said. I had never had tea.

I followed her into the house with only a little trepidation. Her home was cool and warm at the same time, and bursting with daylight that wasn't soaked in red. The carpet wasn't ripped from the floor boards, the walls weren't stained with blood or bruised with water damage. There wasn't a dead body to be found, not anywhere, and I looked pretty hard.

I watched her run water from the sink into a kettle. I stared.

"You haven't seen running water before, have you?" she asked.

I just shook my head.

"What is this place?" I asked.

"Black Hole," she answered. "Oh, don't worry. You'll understand. Besides, it won't last long."

I didn't know what she meant by that.

She smiled at me while she waited for something, and when the tea kettle sang at her, I jumped. She laughed kindly, and poured hot water into two cups. It steamed like the wreckage of the train. I watched her dip two tiny, pretty bags of what looked like dead things into the water, and wrinkled my nose.

"Smell," she said. She held one of the unused bags up to my nose, and I tentatively sniffed it. It was beautiful. It smelled alive. It smelled like the world that once was, the world I would never ever know.

"Nice, isn't it?" she asked.

I had heard of a place where people went when they died. A boy had told me about it, before things got really bad.

"Is this the heaven?" I asked her.

She only smiled at me.

～◎～

We sat on her porch, she in a rocking chair, and me on a swing. There were cushions beneath me, soft and fat, and I felt a little like a prince. I sipped the tea carefully. It burned my lips. I tried to hold the cup the way she did, with the saucer cradled beneath it. I felt awkward and mechanical.

Over the porch rail, across her yard, beyond the fence, I could see the grease field. To the left and right the town unfolded simply, little pleasant houses and shops as well-kept as her own. More than that, there were people everywhere. Not many, but more than I had seen in one place since I was a boy. The railway men were gathered at the edge of the field, hands on their hips, staring at the remains of the train. A woman passed by, holding the hand of a little girl in a bright pink dress. A man flew by on a bicycle.

"I bet you've never seen one of those," the woman said from the rocking chair.

I looked at her. "Not like that."

And it was true. I had seen plenty of bicycles — but they were usually rusted or abandoned, their crumpled metal skeletons wheel-less and forgotten.

"My name is Josie," the woman said. "I've lived here for a few days. What's yours?"

I blinked at her. "A few days?"

She nodded. "We'll get to that. What do I call you?"

I had to think about it. "I can't remember," I said, finally.

"Well, it only seems rude not to call you by a name," she said. "Should we come up with one for you?"

I had never thought about a name. I let her pick. She chose Henry.

"It's my favorite of the names," she said.

"Henry," I repeated.

"It means ruler of the house."

"But I don't have a house," I said.

"Ah," Josie answered. "Well, we'll talk about that, too."

It's starting," she said.

I didn't know what she meant, but she nodded at the field, where the boxcars had been sinking slowly since the crash.

"They're sinking," I said. "I saw earlier."

"Yes, but did you wonder why?"

I shrugged. I looked down and saw that I had finished the tea, and looked around for a place to put the cup and saucer down.

"Let me," Josie said. She took them from me with one hand, and disappeared into the house. The screen door banged shut behind her. From inside the house, I could hear her still talking. "After all," she went on, "have you ever seen a tilled field that soft?"

"I didn't know how soft it was," I said, confused.

The door creaked, then banged shut again as she came back onto the porch.

"It's soft as sand, though it doesn't look it," she said, handing me a cellophane-wrapped white and red disc. "Here. A peppermint."

I looked at it blankly.

"So many new things," she said.

I struggled with the wrapper and she said, "The field looks more substantial than it really is."

We watched as one of the railway men slapped another man on the back, and then the first man jogged out into the field, pointing himself in the direction of the nearest boxcar. The car was more than half-embedded in the soil now, and appeared to be sinking faster than before. It was still slow going, but I could see it happening more clearly than before.

"He probably shouldn't have done that," Josie said.

"Why not? I saw him out there before."

"Well, he won't make it back," she answered. "See? It's going more quickly now."

She was right. Even in the few seconds since the man had climbed onto the roof of the car, things had started sinking faster. The men at the edge of the field noticed, too, and began shouting and waving their arms.

I could hear them: Come back, come back.

But the first man ignored them, and went into the boxcar through its open door. He leaned out again a moment later, holding a folder stuffed with papers. He pointed at it and raised his shoulders questioningly.

The men at the edge of the field became agitated and leaped up and down, but the first man didn't seem to understand. He climbed a short ladder up the boxcar to its roof, and as he did, the car must have found an air pocket somewhere beneath the field, because it lurched and just dropped. I saw the man's eyebrows, tiny fuzzy worms, lift in astonishment, and then he and the car were gone, swallowed up entirely by the field.

The men at the edge of the field shouted and ran around in small circles, throwing their arms around.

"They don't understand," Josie said.

I looked at her. "I don't either."

She leaned forward and patted my knee. "It's okay. In time."

⌒◎⌒

We watched as the rest of the cars disappeared beneath the soil, and for a time things were quiet. The railway men sank to the ground and held their knees to their chests and just stared at the field, and the smoldering train and ripped tracks beyond.

"How come your town looks —"

"Alive?" Josie finished. "Kept-up?"

I nodded.

"Have you ever seen anything like it before?" she asked.

I shook my head. "Just ruins."

"You're still young," she said. "Do you know anything about the world before?"

"Only a little," I said. "What I learn from looking at the mess left behind. My mother told me some things, but I was little."

"Where is she now?"

I shrugged.

"She probably would have had the sickness," Josie said. "Almost all of them did. How old were you when she went away?"

"I don't know."

"You look about nineteen to me," Josie said. "Maybe old for your age, so you fool people into thinking you're twenty-five or so. But I think you're just a kid still."

"I don't know."

"World before was like this," Josie said, waving her hands at the houses. "Not all of it. Not even most of it. But there were people, and most of the buildings were standing upright, and there wasn't the sickness making them ill or crazy or just worn-down. Cars on the roads, planes in the sky. You ever see a plane before?"

"I saw one upside down on a house once," I said. "But when I was really little, I think I remember seeing one or two in the air. Rumor was that's where all the people went, to a town up there that just flies around. I heard someone say once they saw it. I never did."

"That's an interesting rumor," Josie said. "But you know where all the people went. You've seen them, here and there."

"Dead."

"Almost all of them. The ones that are left either work the railroad, or they're like you — drifting, shell-shocked."

"I'm not shell… shell…"

"Shocked," she finished. "I think you are. Why do you ride the trains?"

I thought about it, then looked down. "I don't know what else to do."

"There you have it," Josie said. "Everybody who isn't dead yet feels like that. Purposeless."

"Maybe the trains are going somewhere good," I said, hopefully.

"Maybe," Josie said. "But I think they just run from one side of the coast to the other. I think they're pur-poseless, too. Have you ever seen any cargo on them? Food, or cattle, or anything?"

I shook my head. "I found a book. A few days ago."

"What was it about?" She studied my face. "Oh. You couldn't read it."

"No," I confessed. "There were some drawings."

"What kind?"

"Like someone drew them. I recognized some, like a campfire. Food."

"So it was a journal."

"What's a journal?"

She thought about it. "It's a book that someone

makes and puts their own words into, instead of a book that has words already printed in it."

"It was a journal," I agreed. "I thought maybe it belonged to someone like me. Someone who rode the trains."

"Might have," she said. She nodded. "It really might have. There was a lot of that before things got bad. People hopping the trains like they did in the old, old days. Ride them as far as they'll take you, and maybe you'll get away from the sickness, from the problems. Except the problems were everywhere. They weren't local problems. They were — species problems."

A terrible, wrenching sound interrupted her. Josie clapped her hands and leaned forward.

"Oh, it's starting now," she cried happily. "It's starting!"

✎

I didn't see what she meant, so she pointed. It took a moment, but then I saw it clearly: on one of the houses on the west side of the field, a single board quivered. It was leaning away from the house, one end of it pulled free by some invisible hand. It trembled and shook and creaked loudly, and I could hear a twanging sound that I'd never heard before.

"The nails," Josie said. "Happens when they pop free."

The railway men stood up and pointed. One of them clapped his hands to his head in disbelief. Around them, the people on the streets hurried back into their homes, mothers tugging their children along. The man with the bicycle passed again, battling the pedals as if pushing into a stiff wind. And that's when I noticed that the board on the side of the blue house wasn't the only thing being pulled at. Everything was being pulled. The trees that I could see, rich with leaves like I'd never seen, were bending towards the grease field. Their leaves went first, plucked away by a force I couldn't name if I tried. Then they all went, and a storm of beautiful green and golden leaves swirled through the air, toward the field.

"What's happening?" I asked.

"Look," Josie said.

The leaves swooped like a flock of swallows, twisting and coming together and separating again, and then with tremendous force they bolted for the field. The sound that a million leaves make when they hit the ground at the same time is the same as a building collapsing. The field was immediately blanketed with them, and the force of their landing almost knocked the railway men over.

"There they go," Josie said, pointing.

The field swallowed them in great clumps, drawing them down beneath the soil quickly and with a sucking sound. I could feel the ground beneath us vibrate at that sound, feel the chains in the porch swing hum with electricity.

And then the leaves were gone, as if they'd never been there at all. The trees still leaned toward the field, tilting at impossible angles, heaving and cracking, roots tearing up from the earth, but they did so bare, their branches like knobby finger bones casting a spell on the field.

"What is happening?"

Josie didn't seem to hear me. "It happens fast, once it starts."

She was right. The largest of the trees resisted, for a while, but the smaller ones were torn from the ground easily, and I watched in disbelief as they slid along the grass and dirt towards the field, their branches seeming to claw for purchase, anything to hold on to. They slid past the railway men — who I noticed were beginning to lean backwards, even if they hadn't noticed it yet — and then the field grasped a branch and just pulled the trees right into it. They sank and disappeared, and then there were raw dirty wounds all over the town where trees once stood.

"What is happening?" I asked again.

It got louder then, as more boards began to bend away from the houses, as bricks were pulled right out of the foundations of buildings. The ground shook, and I could see now that the railway men were terrified. They were trying to run away from the field, but almost comically seemed to be stuck in place, running nowhere desperately. They shouted, and then they fell down, and just like the trees they were hauled over the ground, the rough earth scratching their faces until they bled — and then the men, too, were sucked down into the black soil.

I yelled, I think, and Josie moved from the rocking chair to the swing beside me.

"It's okay," she said to me, patting my knee once more. "Let's go inside."

~⚬~

She poured a fresh cup of tea, but I couldn't drink it.

"I don't understand what's happening," I said.

"Have you ever seen a person get sick and die?" she asked me. "Watched them get a cough first, and then get sicker, and then struggle for weeks, and then just give up?"

"I don't know anybody well enough to see that happen." I looked around at her house, which was quiet and calm and still. Outside I could still hear the war that seemed to be happening. I could hear the houses being ripped and chewed, windows shattering like candy shells. "I want to get out of here."

"Well, you probably could," she said. "If you really wanted to."

I stood up, and she just looked at me calmly.

"What about you?" I said.

"Oh, I couldn't leave."

"But something bad is happening."

"I can see why someone might think it's bad," she answered patiently. "But it's quite good. And anyway, I'm here for a reason. I couldn't leave if I wanted to. I've got no place to go."

I looked around her house. "Why isn't your house coming apart like the others?"

"Well, that's one of the perks of my reason for being here," she said. "Are you sure you won't drink your tea?"

"Why do I hurt right now?" I asked. Because I did. I felt like someone had shoved an iron pipe through my torso until it stuck out at both ends, and now they were beginning to twist it clockwise.

"Tension," she said. "This is a stressful event for some. Here, sit."

She patted the sofa, and I sat down, reluctantly, confused by the noise outside. Josie put her hands gently on my shoulders and began to knead them. I felt a strange crawling sensation and realized that all of the hairs on my arms and neck were standing up. I felt warm. I had never been touched by anyone before. Not even by my mother.

"You'll feel better soon," she said.

I jumped up. "I don't want to get eaten by — by whatever that is!"

"Henry," she said gently. "Please sit down."

~◎~

J osie called it the quick death. She talked about a sick person again, and said that the sickness of the world was just like that. All the destruction and people losing their heads and sense of meaning — all of that was the world becoming ill. It sweated and shivered and we felt all of it. And now the world was dying, and that was what was happening out there.

"I'm going to die," I said.

"Maybe," she said.

"I haven't done anything at all," I said. "Why was I even here?"

"Most people have a lifetime to consider those questions, to do something about them," Josie answered. "You were perhaps unfortunate. You were born during the sick time. You never really had a chance."

"How do you even know all of this?"

"Everything is a cycle," Josie said. "This has happened before. I was there."

I stared at her. "The world has died before," I repeated. "You're scaring me."

"When the world dies, everything goes away," she said. "The board is cleared off so that the next game can begin. Except the board has to go, too, because the game might be a different thing entirely the next time. Maybe the next time the world won't be round, for example. Maybe it will be a ribbon, or maybe it will be a great beast that swims through the river of time. Can you imagine?"

I opened my mouth, then closed it again.

"When the world dies, a witness must be present," Josie said. "That's me. I show up just before it happens. This little town? I made it, just because I like things to be — homey, I guess you might say. It makes me feel better about what's happening."

"A witness," I croaked.

"Right," she said. "The last time that the world died, I was a fish. I had big feathery wings and a purple, bulbous light embedded in my forehead. The world was a very different place last time. You might have liked it, Henry."

"You're crazy," I said. "I just want to get on the train and —"

She got up and walked to the window. "I'm afraid the train is just about gone," she said.

I peered out beside her. It was just about gone. Even as I watched, the last of the cars were pulled apart and drawn into the field. There was a sonorous metallic rippling sound, then, and I asked Josie what it was.

She pointed. The tracks themselves had come free of the ties, and were being slurped into the dark field like long steel noodles. The field was full of things that I hadn't seen fall into it. There was an entire house, up-ended and sinking quickly, with a woman and a man in the windows, just staring back at me. A shining silver automobile, wheels up, gone. A swingset. A mailbox. And at least a dozen people were there, too, fighting against the suction that pulled them below the earth.

Already the town seemed half-gone.

"It takes a little while," Josie said, pulling the curtains shut. "First the immediate area goes. In a few hours, all the buildings that I put here will be gone. The trees, the wheat fields, the picket fences, the schools and playgrounds, the post office. All gone."

"Why did you make the town if it was only going to —"

"Oh, fuel, of course," she answered. "It needs an appetizer to get worked up for the really hard part."

"What do you mean, the hard part?" I asked slowly.

"The board has to be cleared," she repeated. "That means everything."

～◎～

Phoenix, Arizona," she said. "The Statue of Liberty. Those lovely wharves in San Francisco. The Alps. Antarctica. All of it."

"I — you — it just eats it all?"

"Well, I wouldn't think of it as eating, really," Josie said. "It's more like the field is the box that the game pieces go into. And they're just all being swept in. Well, pulled in."

"But what about your house? What about you?" I stopped. "What about me?"

"You saw my nice fence when you came in," she said. "Everything inside that fence stays until the very end. Remember, I'm the witness. I can't witness anything if I'm not here, can I."

"Couldn't everybody just have come to your house, then?"

"Well, no, not really," she said. "Only the ones I invite in. And really, they all know that. Nobody begrudges me this. After all, that they're here at all is a sort of gift, isn't it. They got to enjoy a few days of being alive and muddling about in a pretty little town."

"Where did they come from?"

Josie smiled. "They're just bits and pieces left over from the last time."

I pressed my palms against my eyes.

"You poor dear," she said. "It's a terrible burden to know any of this. Please, have some of your tea. Do you want a cookie?"

"Why did you bring me here?" I asked. "Why did you tell me any of this?"

She smiled again. "Dear, I didn't bring you here. The train did."

◦⊚◦

I slept on the couch for a time, and when I woke up, she said, "Come see."

She was at the window. Her house was still brightly lit and warm, as if the sun lingered right outside, just for her, but beyond the windows the world was barren. The earth had been scraped clean of grass and weeds and rocks until there was only a raw brown surface in every direction. The field seemed larger, felt deeper.

"See?" she asked me, pointing at the horizon.

It took a moment, but then I saw movement, a rippling seam of darkness heading for the field.

"And there," she said, pointing to the east.

I saw many of them then, and realized with a slow, dawning horror that these were caravans of things. Cars, buildings, airplanes, museums, people, swimming pools, and a dense, writhing mass of debris.

"That's all of it," she said. "Watch awhile, and you can say you've seen the world."

"All of it," I said. "You mean —"

"I mean every single thing sitting above or below the surface of this earth. Every oil well, every bird, every buried treasure, every casket, every street sign, every brick from every bridge ever built. I always feel a bit sad for the people, though. They don't usually survive the trip. They're very fragile."

The streams arrived hours later, and I watched as they poured into the field. It swelled to accommodate the magnitude of the objects, until the field covered the earth as far as I could see. Enormous freight ships and airport signal towers sank into the soil, buckling and crumpling like aluminum foil.

"It's getting so big," I said.

"Eventually it doesn't have to suck anything in," Josie explained. "Eventually it gets big enough that everything just sinks on its own, and then it's over pretty fast. After that — well, wait and see."

～⊙～

After that, the universe followed.

It started with the clouds. Josie woke me from another nap to show me a fat white cloud thrashing in the center of the field. I watched as more and more of them fell from the sky, watched as the sky itself thinned and turned black. The moon grew larger and larger and larger and then just vanished. I looked at Josie.

"Well, you could say that the field has become the biggest planet in the solar system now," she said, "although that's not strictly true. It's a useful metaphor, though. Think of it like this — was the moon sucked in? Or did the field just get so big that it bumped into the moon?"

I looked around. Her house seemed untouched. Every crocheted blanket and framed photograph was in place. The porch swing outside swayed idly on its chains. The teapot sang again in the kitchen.

"What happens after that?" I asked.

"Well," she said, calling over her shoulder from the kitchen, "the field expands and expands and expands. All the planets that you knew, they go away. Jupiter, Neptune, all of those. Your sun."

"It eats the sun?"

"It eats everything," she said. "Planets and stars are enormously stimulating, so it gets even faster after that, and before long, it's entire galaxies, and then it catches up to the expanding universe, and then it's all over."

I stared at the cup in her hand.

"More tea?" she asked.

"It's not really a field, is it," I said.

She shook her head. "Nothing is ever really anything. It just looks like something. When it all starts over, it will be something different, unlike anything you've ever seen before."

I took a deep breath. "And what about me?"

"Well," Josie answered, "when it's big enough to

start over, it needs something to start over with. That's you."

I felt very heavy. "Me."

"You," she said again. "Tea, Henry."

~⊙~

Days passed, I think, and then there was a faint popping sound, and Josie sat up straight.

"Well," she said, "that's it, then."

We walked onto the porch. Beyond her green lawn and careful flower garden and nice picket fence posts there was only whiteness. Pure, blank white, as though the world had stumbled into the a thicket of clouds.

"It's white," I said.

"What did you expect it to be?"

"Black," I said. "I guess."

"Well, I suppose you can make it whatever you like," she answered. "If black is what you prefer, then black is what it shall be."

"What do you mean?"

"I can't tell you anything more," Josie said. "It's time for you to go."

"Go?" I felt my stomach lurch. "Where do I go? What's going to happen to me?"

She took my hand and walked with me down the steps to the cobblestone path, and led me to the gate. She patted my hand and said, "The rest is for you. I can't help you any longer. Just call me when you need me."

"Need you?" I said. "I need you now. I want another cup of tea. A cookie. I'm sleepy. I need a nap. My body aches."

"Henry," she said sweetly, and then she opened the gate.

I felt a faint suction, and fear flooded my veins. I was lifted off of my feet and drawn through the gate and into the whiteness. Josie and her house fell away from me slowly, and she waved, then turned and went back into her house. The fence folded over, and folded over again, and the lawn and the steps and the house followed suit, until Josie and her home and everything around me were gone.

The sucking sensation dissipated, and I hung alone in the white. I don't know how much time passed, or if any passed at all, or if time was something that existed any longer. I closed my eyes, blind to all sensations. There were no smells, no breezes to be felt.

I thought of strawberries.

Strawberries on the night air, and a plump white moon in a dark blue blanket. The smell of cinders and coal. Boxcars that were dry and stuffed with hay, drawn along behind mighty engines that sailed through quiet, sleepy towns and patchwork farmland and dark, burbling rivers. A burlap sack to keep me warm, the sway of the train to lull me to sleep, and maybe a journal to write in.

I was the last of the rail-riders.

I am the first of all things.

I opened my eyes, and it was so.

THE
DARK AGE

THEN

I caught her.

The doctor gave me a textured blue wrap. Frannie looked alarmed and said, "No, no, skin — skin-to-skin, I want skin-to-skin," and the doctor assured her that this was only for me, so that I wouldn't drop her. I lost track of what I was supposed to feel, and I bent over the bed, only dimly aware of Frannie's feet near my head, her toes splayed wide as she fought. I heard her scream like I'd never heard her do anything before. It was primal, and I felt like a hunter on the savannah, standing over my kill, like a warrior, head thrown back and the taste of blood in my mouth.

And then she came to me, like a child on a water slide into my arms, slippery and dark and blue, and I caught her, and her tiny face looked like the wrinkles of my knee, almost featureless in her surprise, and she bawled rapidly. She pierced my heart and my ears with her cries, and a nurse clamped and clipped the cord, and I carried her to Frannie and laid our daughter on her breast.

She wailed and clung to her mother, her tiny fingers opening and closing against Frannie's skin, and Frannie breathed heavily and said, "Elle."

I didn't want to look away from either of them — Frannie dripping with sweat, her hair in damp rings on her face, and Elle, pushing against her mother's skin like a fresh piglet — but the movement at the door caught my eye, and I did, I looked up, and for the rest of my life I wished that I hadn't.

Frannie saw, and looked, too.

The man in the doorway smiled regretfully, and waggled his fingers at me, and nodded.

I met Frannie's dark eyes, and watched the tears well up, and I felt my heart pull out of my chest and stay behind in that beautiful room, the most wonderful place that had ever been made. I kissed Frannie, but she kissed me back, harder, and then I nuzzled Elle's tiny soft ear with my nose, and kissed her head everywhere, and her small hands. I would have stayed in the room forever if I could have.

But I followed the man out of the room, my ears ringing with sadness, an enormous hole in my head and my heart, and that was that. We both knew that it had to happen, but we pretended it wasn't going to. And then it did.

I followed his dark suit through the hospital corridor. I couldn't feel my hands. My feet moved on their own.

He said something, but I don't know what it was.

We stepped out of the building and into the light, and the cold wind turned my tears to ice.

NOW

Elle taps the camera, and I watch her fingertip, large enough to crush worlds, grow dark and obscure my view. I laugh, and she giggles, and this makes her laugh harder, and then she begins to hiccup wildly. She rocks back on her bottom and puts her hands on the floor behind her, and reclines and stares at me, hiccuping and laughing, and I laugh with her.

"You're silly," I say to her. "Silly, silly Elle."

She babbles at me, and in the stream of muddled sounds I hear something that sounds like *a-da*, and I say, "Frannie!"

Frannie turns the camera on herself, and her smile is big and bright and threatens to push her eyes off of her face. "We've been working on it all week," she says. "She can't quite make the d sound work, so all we've got is *ada-ada*, except, you know, it's more like *atha, atha*."

I turn away from the camera and wipe at my eyes.

"Daddy's crying," Frannie says. I look back to see

her turn the camera to Elle, who thinks this is hilarious. She pats her round tummy and laughs harder, and then the hiccups take over in a big way, and a moment later Elle burps up breakfast.

"Oh, uh-oh! Uh-oh!" Frannie sing-songs, and she says to me, "We'll be right back, Daddy!" and puts the camera down.

I watch Frannie's feet, then she scoops up Elle and whisks her out of frame.

I sigh and push off of the wall and turn in a slow flip, waiting.

Sarah comes in through the research wing hatch and sees the camera and says, "Oh, shit — I mean — oh, *goddammit*, I — fuck! Shit."

I laugh at her and tell her it's fine. "Elle spit up," I say. "Commercial break."

Her face relaxes. "Whew. Okay. I don't want to corrupt your little girl or anything."

"Did I forget to flip the sign?"

Sarah turns around and leans out of sight. "Well — nope, no, you did," she says, leaning back in and holding up the little handwritten recording sign. "I wasn't even looking, I guess."

"What did you need?"

She looks around, scatter-brained, gathering her thoughts. Then Frannie comes back into the room with Elle, singing a bit, and she sees Sarah on the display and says, "Sarah! Hi!"

Sarah looks up at the screen and smiles sheepishly. "Hi, Francine," she says.

"Everything okay?" Frannie asks me.

"Everything's fine," I say.

"I was — I shouldn't be in here," Sarah says, making a slow turn towards the hatch. "I'm sorry. Nice to see you, Francine."

"Bye, Sarah," Frannie says. She lifts Elle's small hand and flaps it at the camera. "Say 'Bye, Sarah!'"

Elle yawns.

"Bye, sweetie," Sarah says, then shakes her head at herself and looks at me. "Really, I'm sorry. I'm sorry. I should've checked first."

"Not a big deal," I say, and then Sarah floats back into the research module and presses the hatch shut behind her.

"It's not like we were having phone sex," Frannie says, chuckling. "Make sure she knows it's fine."

I look at the readout beside the screen. "Time's up anyway," I say.

Frannie's frown is adorable. "Oh, I'm sorry, dear," she says. "We wasted so much time cleaning Elle up — I'm so sorry."

I smile, but I know it's a sad smile, and I know Frannie can tell. "Kiss her for me," I say.

Frannie kisses Elle, a big playful smooch that sets Elle's giggles off again.

"Love," I say.

"Love," Frannie answers, and then she squeezes Elle and coos, "Love! Love!"

The screen goes dark, and I sigh, and look around the module. It's cramped and small, but it's private, at least until Sarah bumbles in again. I point my hands at the floor and push off with my feet, just enough to reach the lights, and I snap them off. The module goes pitch-black, and then my eyes adjust to the faint light from the porthole. And then I cry, the way I always do. The tears stick to my face like film, and when I've cried enough to feel better, I sop them up with my sleeve, and turn on the lights, and get back to work.

~∘~

This is the way it has to be.

I was already in the program when Frannie and I met. She sometimes asked me that awful, difficult question: Would I have signed up for this if we'd already been married? And I tell her no, of course I wouldn't, but I would have. I still would have. Some things are important, and then some things resonate through history like a bell, and this is one of those resonant things, being here, aboard the *Arecibo*, crawling through the night.

Then Frannie got pregnant, despite our best efforts and multiple contraceptives, and my answer to that question softened.

When I caught Elle that morning in the hospital room, I knew that it had changed. Frannie saw it on my face, I think, though we have never talked about it since then. But she knew that my heart had changed, and by noticing that, she learned that my earlier answers had been kind lies.

We are a crew of seven, with the simplest of orders.
See what's out there.

So that's what we're doing.

We've all left something behind.

It isn't easy for any of us.

We are martyrs.

I think of Elle's bright eyes and her shock of blonde hair, and I wonder what it would feel like to hold her, that hair tickling my face as she falls asleep on my shoulder.

I would hold her for hours and hours and never grow tired.

It wouldn't matter to me if my arms fell off.

Every day I grow heavier with regret.

Every day I hate my younger, star-crossed self a little more.

※

Sarah is the scientist. Introverted, awkward, a little odd.

Then there's Mikael, our technician. We wanted to call him an engineer, but he prefers *spaceship guy*. As in, "Hey, spaceship guy, the wing just fell off."

Stefan and Heidi are the pilots. Heidi has a secondary specialty — she's the shrink.

I'm the communications guy.

Walter is the physician and nutritionist. Edith is the researcher.

They are all quite nice.

We have a pact among us — an unwritten one, one that the WSA probably figured would happen but did not write into our training manuals, or account for during our isolation boot camp in Antarctica — that anybody can sleep with anybody else, and nobody will be jealous, and that our families on Earth will never know. It was Walter's suggestion. Heidi thought it was a marvelous idea, and would reduce tension. So far I think Mikael and Edith have been together, and Walter and Stefan, and the plan has held water. But I think soon someone will feel bad, and then things will be strange.

I told Frannie about the pact. It was our first video chat. She thought it made sense, and told me that she couldn't begrudge me for taking part.

"Sarah seems nice," Frannie had said.

"I don't want to sleep with anyone else," I told Frannie. "I miss you."

"Be practical," Frannie said. "We're talking about the rest of your life here. You aren't a monk. You shouldn't be."

Heidi approached me a few days later. I said no, and she wasn't upset or embarrassed. I didn't tell Frannie. I don't know why I didn't.

∽✺∽

We have all left something behind, somehow. We talk about these things, about our families and lovers, as if it will somehow ease the pain of it all. Mikael had just met his birth parents for the first time. He thinks it would have been easier to never have met them, but Walter thought that it was better to know. "Now you won't spend the rest of your life wondering about it," he said to Mikael once.

Heidi has a husband and two children. They're in college. Her husband writes novels. She thinks that he'll be happier alone. She doesn't talk about her children. Each of us keeps something for ourselves, and doesn't talk about it.

I am just like a new father on Earth. Each time Frannie sends me a video of Elle doing something new, I show everyone. Stefan seems the most enthusiastic about her progress. Edith always watches and nods, and then goes back to what she was doing before. I don't care. I sometimes wonder if I must share Elle with everybody so that everybody will recognize the enormity of my personal loss. I told Heidi that during one of our sessions, once.

Heidi said, "Is that what you think?"

Of all of them, Sarah is the closest to a friend for me. She seems to like Frannie, and that makes me like Sarah more. I like that she doesn't talk much, that she prefers to be alone. I like that she considers me the next best thing to being alone.

Sarah seems nice.

Sometimes I think about it.

∽◎∾

Elle gets bigger and bigger. Frannie and I celebrate Elle's birthdays every month, to make up for the many I will miss. The WSA permits only two communications per week, and I look forward to them as much as I did to my own birthdays as a child.

I miss every first.

Frannie will wait for my call, then excitedly tell me that Elle has started walking, that she had her first solid food, that she said her first word. Elle demonstrates all of these things for me, but I feel like one of my shipmates — not a parent, but an audience. I cry every time. The emptiness between us feels incalculably large, larger every time we talk. I see Elle's eyes change from blue to green, her chubby cheeks become slim, her hair fall to her shoulders. She wears the clothes of an adult — pretty sweaters and thick tights and patent shoes, and I feel a terrible fear seize me when I realize what is coming.

Frannie sees it in my face. She doesn't know what to say. She only says, "We love you more than anything." She means it, but I can feel the helplessness behind her words.

The inevitability of the *Arecibo* launch hung over our pregnancy like a pall, like a storm that grew darker and more ominous every day.

But it is nothing like the storm that approaches now.

∼☙∽

The WSA has mandated special counseling sessions for each of you," Heidi says over breakfast a few days later. "Now, I'm inclined to agree — but I'd like you all to tell me if you prefer them to be one-on-ones, or if you would consider a group session."

She studies everyone's faces, and when nobody speaks, she adds, "I think a group session would be more productive."

Everybody dreads the Long Sleep, as they've been calling it. Walter says it's not exactly a Sleep. "It's a dark age," he says. "Literally, it's *the* Dark Age."

Heidi looks around the room and says, "Right. Okay. A group session."

～☾～

Sarah sits beside me. We're all gathered at the dining table in the galley. There aren't many chairs aboard the *Arecibo* that aren't attached to consoles, so the galley was the default choice. One by one the crew floats in and buckles themselves into a seat at the table. Heidi comes in and sits down and says, "Who are we missing?"

"Edith," Mikael offers.

"Is she coming?" Heidi asks.

Mikael shakes his head. "She doesn't want to talk about it."

Heidi sighs, and thinks about this, then says, "Alright. We're on our own out here, folks. WSA can't really do anything to you. Does anybody else want to skip this?"

Silence, and then Stefan unbuckles and leaves. Mikael shrugs apologetically, then follows.

We watch them go.

"So," Walter says cheerily.

Heidi smiles at him and I wonder if they've slept together.

"The Long Sleep," Heidi says.

"The Dark Age," Walter contradicts.

"Whatever. How do you all feel? Who wants to talk about it first?"

I begin to cry immediately.

Sarah pats my knee beneath the table, then leaves her hand there, and I feel my skin flush hot.

Sarah seems nice.

"Maybe this should really be mandatory," Walter suggests.

※

Frannie is exhausted. She's alone on the screen, her eyes rimmed red. Her hair is disheveled, and she's wearing her pajamas.

"Frannie?" I ask.

She tells me about her day — Elle has been throwing tantrums, but it's because she has a fever, Frannie thinks, so she's trying to remain as patient as she can, but it's wearing her down. Elle hasn't slept more than a half-hour for two days. "Can you hear her?" Frannie asks.

"Yes," I say. The sound of my daughter crying hundreds of thousands of miles away is wrenching. I want to go to her. I want to pick her up and hold her close and say, "It's okay, Daddy's here." I want her to snuggle close and sniffle herself to sleep in my arms.

Frannie says, "It's so hard," and she cries.

"Fran," I say, leaning close to the camera. "Darling."

"I'm so alone," she says.

I strap myself into my bunk that night and think about my sins.

I have abandoned them.

I hate myself.

I unstrap and go to Heidi.

"What if I killed myself?" I ask her.

~◦◎◦~

The Long Sleep, the Dark Age. One hundred forty-four years of hibernation sleep. Autopilot. Essential systems and life support only. Seven people, quietly stored in airtight sleeves in a module with countless systems redundancies. Heart rates slowed and monitored. Data transmitted daily back to Earth, for a long slow journey to the WSA's computers for analysis and modulation.

"Well, you shouldn't do that," Heidi says.

"Tell me why," I demand. I'm crying. I'm the most unstable person on the *Arecibo*, I think.

"Because your wife and daughter would know,"

Heidi says.

She doesn't have to say another word.

But she does.

"If you want to kill yourself when we wake up," Heidi says, "then at least you won't hurt them."

⁓◉⁓

The possibilities are impossible to predict. The WSA and our native governments have put in place a series of treaties and contingencies, and written a strange new constitutional document that will take effect should any one of those bodies no longer exist when we wake up. A lot can happen in a century and a half. We might wake to find that the WSA has lost its funding. There might have been wars. Earth could have been destroyed by a meteor. Or it might have evolved into a technological utopia. The cure for death might have been discovered, in which case our families might survive to see us again.

But nobody knows for sure.

Frannie says, "What am I supposed to do?"

"What do you mean?"

Elle sits on Frannie's lap, playing with a toy I don't recognize, a plush character from a children's show, and it strikes me again that I am left out of even Elle's tiniest experiences. Does she hold that doll close when she sleeps? Is it her favorite?

"Am I supposed to be alone for the rest of my life, too?" she asks.

I don't know what to say to her.

"I'm sorry," she says, wiping her eyes. "I didn't know it was going to be this hard."

"I'm an asshole," I say.

Her eyes widen and she looks in Elle's direction, then back at me.

"I'm sorry," I say. "Elle, ignore Daddy."

Frannie turns the camera to Elle's face. "Say night-night to Daddy," she says.

My beautiful daughter looks up and smiles and says, "Nigh-nigh, Daddy."

Frannie turns the camera back to her own lovely face and says, "I'm sorry. Don't worry about us. We're going to be just fine. We love you."

"I love you, too," I say, and kiss my fingers and hold them up to Frannie's.

❧

Sarah is in the research module when I come out.

"I thought everyone was asleep," I say.

She shrugs. "Sorry. Sometimes I can't sleep. Are you okay?"

I touch my face. My skin is tight. "I was crying," I say. "I'm fine."

"You're a sweet man," Sarah says to me.

"I wanted to kill myself."

She smiles sadly. "We all do."

I float past her and go through the hatch to our sleeping quarters, and then I turn and look back at her.

"I'm putting her through so much," I say. "It's inhuman. I can't think of anything worse."

"I can think of lots worse," Sarah says. "But Frannie's wonderful. She'll be okay. She'll find someone."

I look down.

"You have to let her do that," Sarah says. "You're not really hers any more. She's not really yours."

"I — yeah."

"I don't know what it feels like to be in your skin," she says. "But maybe it helps if you think of them as a story that you're watching. Like on television."

"I'm going to miss every episode," I say.

She nods. "But you'll know the ending tomorrow."

I can't help it. I cry. The thought of my family growing up, growing *old,* dying — and that all of it will happen while I'm asleep — feels like someone has grabbed my ribs and is spreading them apart, pulling as hard as a body can be pulled. It feels like I'm going to come apart, and I double over involuntarily.

Sarah is there, then, and she holds me and we wobble in zero-gravity together. She puts her hand on my face, and my tears crawl from my skin to hers.

"You won't lose everything," she whispers. "I'll be here when you wake up."

⚓

The last conversation with Frannie is surreal. She is wearing the bulky sweater that I liked, the one with the neck that is wide enough for her shoulder to peek through. I stare at her skin and try to remember what it felt like to touch it. I try to remember her smell. I can't.

Elle is wearing a beautiful sundress and yellow rain boots. "Boots!" she cries, pointing at them.

"Boots," I agree, trying not to cry again.

Frannie smiles with shining eyes as Elle runs to her toy chest and picks up a building block, then brings it to the camera.

"Block!" she says. Her eyes are big and she bites her lip, waiting for me to understand.

"Block," I say, nodding.

I wish that I could stack the blocks with her into a great big prison cell, and stay inside of it forever with her. I watch her run to the toy chest. She puts the block down and picks up a squeaky giraffe.

"Raffe!" she says, displaying it to the camera.

"Giraffe," I say.

"Elle, honey," Frannie says as Elle runs back to her toys. "Daddy has to go in a minute. Can you say goodbye? Can you tell him how much you love him?"

I cannot hold back my tears. I suck in deep breaths and stare longingly at the Earthbound room and my girls inside of it.

"I miss you, Ellie," I choke out.

"Daddy misses you," Frannie says.

Elle comes back to the camera and holds up a stuffed pig. "Piggie!" she cries.

I nod like a fool, and she runs away again. Frannie snatches her up and brings her back to the camera, and

Elle kicks in protest, and Frannie looks at the camera with a terrible fear in her eyes and says, "I'm sorry, I'm sorry, she's —"

The digital counter beside the screen runs out, and the screen goes dark.

❧

Heidi and Walter see to us all, one by one. Walter will be the last into the units, as the ship's doctor.

He stands in front of me, adjusting the monitoring belt. He is close enough that I can feel his breath. He smells like coffee. He smiles at me and says, "It's going to be a pleasant dream. Okay?"

I nod and look away, uncomfortable at his closeness.

Heidi comes by next, after attending to Sarah, who will be in the sleeve beside mine.

"Are you okay?" she asks.

I am tired of crying. I feel as if I have cried a thousand years.

"The first thing Walter's going to do is adjust the gas compounds in your sleeve," she says. "There's a light neuro-sedative in the mix. You'll feel relaxed and care-free."

"I don't want to sleep," I say.

"We all have to," she says.

"I'll stay awake. I'll watch over the ship, make sure everything runs fine. I'll make sure you'll all be okay."

"The ship can do that for itself," Heidi says. She

leans closer and kisses my forehead. "You are going to be alright. When you wake, we'll talk. Okay?"

I think about Heidi's family. "What about your kids?" I ask. "Don't you care about them?"

She is unruffled by my tone. "My boys will be fine," she says.

"They got to know their mom," I say bitterly.

Heidi's smile is kinder than I deserve. "Let me help you inside," she says.

∽☙∾

Inside the sleeve is a slim, curved screen. It is fixed to the thick polyglass before my eyes, and it displays a simple message.

You are humanity's finest, it says. *We wish you godspeed and long lives. Make us all proud. — WSA, Earth*

The message disappears, replaced by something new.

Hey. Look left.

I frown, then turn my head.

Sarah waves at me in the clear sleeve next to mine. She says something, but I can't hear her, and I shake my head. I mouth, "I can't hear you."

She points at the screen in front of her face. I understand, and look back at mine.

The message reads, *We can talk until we fall asleep.*

Then another line: *It's voice-activated. Just talk.*

I say, "Hi."

Hi.

I look over at Sarah — weird, strange Sarah — and she smiles.

"You're too happy," I say.

You're the saddest person I've ever met.

"I should be," I say back. "I'm a monster."

Will you be okay?

I hear a dim hissing sound, and outside the sleeve Walter waves at me, then gives me a thumbs-up. He folds his hands beside his face and mimes falling asleep. I nod blankly at him, and then he moves on.

It smells sweet.

I sniff the air. "I don't want it."

I know you're scared. You're a good man.

"I'm not. I'm not a good man."

You're not really the best judge of character. Your own, I mean.

"Sarah," I say, feeling the drift of the gases. "I'm terrified."

It will be over before you know it.

"That's what I mean. When I wake up, my little Elle —"

She will be proud of her daddy. What do all the other dads do that's so special?

"She'll hate me," I say. "She'll die thinking I left her, that I didn't love her."

She knows.

I stare at the screen. To my left, Sarah is drifting.

I say, "Record a message."

❦

*E*lle, Frannie —
      I hope with all of my heart that this message comes through. Maybe the WSA will see it and make sure. I hope so.

We're going to sleep now. It's about to happen — I already feel woozy. I'm sorry. This is my last message and I'm going to sound like a drunk. I'm sorry, I'm so sorry —

Frannie, my dear, my sweet wife. I have loved you since I met you. I wish that I could hold you forever, but I can't — I have to let you go. Be happy. Fill your days with love. Fill Elle's.

Elle, sweetheart — I'm going to cry, I'm sorry — Elle, there is nothing — I — oh, god, I'm drifting, it's happening —

Elle — Elle —

I hold you always.

I am — I am always —

Elle —

∽◉∾

*T*he message ends, and I blink away tears.
      "Stupid," I whisper to myself. "I didn't say anything at all."

Sarah is wrapped in a white blanket beside me. Her eyes are wet, too.

"You said everything," she says. "Everything."

We sit in shock around the table with the others. Each of us leans on another.

Heidi looks the worst, as if she can't believe it's real. "My pretty boys," she whispers.

The table is lit from within, a soft bone-blue glow

like a ghost, which is exactly what it is. Before each of us are the messages we sent to our families and loved ones — except for Stefan's. He presses his palms hard to his eyes. Walter rubs his back.

"I didn't know," Stefan rasps, his voice tired from the years of sleep.

"He didn't send any messages," Sarah whispers.

I nod. What a terrible feeling for his family on Earth — to wait for his message, to see reports of the others and their final letters, and to never receive their own.

Poor Stefan.

A gentle tone sounds, and I look down at the table.

2,783 messages retrieved.

"What's this?" I ask.

"You're the communications specialist," Mikael says.

∽⊘∾

2,783 messages.

The sum total of missives sent to the *Arecibo* from Earth following our entry into the Long Sleep. Most are reports from the WSA — status updates on major events. It is an otherworldly feeling, thumbing through them and seeing tiny bites of history. They read like fictions: *North Korea. Nuclear detonation. Dissolved democracy.* It's like reading an alternate history, a science fiction novel.

The WSA is gone, we learn. The World Space Association was disbanded in 2142 — "They couldn't have waited until we woke up?" Walter asks — which explains the dead air on the networks.

The United States is gone as well.

"All empires fall," says Heidi, but she says it in a haunted voice.

The rest of the messages are personal ones.

Sarah has dozens from her parents. Heidi's boys have recorded hours of video — she is a grandmother. Each of the crew has countless messages. Stefan has many, and this seems to cheer him.

I have one.

༄༅

It's a video.

I don't recognize her at first. Her blonde hair is brown now, her green eyes steady. She is outdoors, at a picnic table. The sky is pink behind her — dawn over the trees. She's backlit, partially in rose-colored shadow. She stares into the camera, and opens her mouth once, then twice, as if she isn't sure where to begin. A nervous smile, and I see her then: I see her mother in her upside-down smile, the smile that should by all rights be a frown but isn't. I see myself in her eyes. She is older than I am now.

Elle.

Nine hours of video.

"Daddy," she says, looking straight into the camera. Her voice is strong and a little scratchy, like her mother's.

I remember her wrinkled pink skin, her insignificant

weight in my hands. Her strange smell, her little fish mouth gasping at the air.

"Boots!"

Her tiny fingers, opening, closing.

A-da.

A tear slides down her cheek. I am struck by her beauty and how much of an adult she has become. I have so many questions for her, and I will never be able to ask any of them.

"I hold you always," she says, repeating my own confused words back to me.

Her tears spill over, and so do mine, my long sleep over, my dark age turned to light.

AFTERWORD

Thanks so much for reading *Deep Breath Hold Tight*. This is not a book that I expected to publish this year. When January came around there were just two projects on my radar: *Eleanor*, the novel I've been trying to finish for fourteen years, and *The Travelers*, the final book in my *Movement* series. Then I surprised myself by writing a whole lot of short stories, something I haven't done in years. This book is a collection of those stories. From cover to cover, this book was pure joy to write. I hope you felt the same way about reading it.

This collection of short stories is dedicated to a special person. Jan Gruhn taught a creative writing class at my high school in Anchorage, Alaska, in the

1990s. She saw something in me, and in my writing, and allowed me to exist outside of her lesson plans, writing short story after short story for class credit. She fueled a small fire that's still roaring today, and I owe her an awful lot for that. Dedicating this collection of short stories to her is a small thing. (Mrs. Gruhn, if you ever happen to read this book, I hope it's worth at least a B-plus.)

Each of the short stories in this book has appeared somewhere else previously: *Wolf Skin, The Caretaker, The Last Rail-Rider* and *The Dark Age* were each self-published individually in the first few months of 2014. *The Winter Lands* appeared in *From the Indie Side,* a speculative fiction anthology edited by David Gatewood. And finally, *Onyx* and *Nebulae* are short excerpts from the first two novels in my *Movement* series, *The Settlers* and *The Colonists,* respectively. Each was self-published in 2013 as a limited-time preview of each novel.

Short stories have an advantage over the novel, I think, and that may be why I've written so many of them this winter and spring. (They're also likely a distraction from *Eleanor,* the novel I seem incapable of completing.) In a novel, readers expect a certain answer – closure, of sorts, to the tale that they've invested so much time and energy in.

But in a short story there are no such expectations. Ambiguity is not anathema to the short story, so when I write one, I find myself stepping away from the microphone just before the final note plays. Many of the short stories in this novel leave much of their final acts to the reader to interpret as he or she may. There's both joy and pain in that for a reader, a fact I'm not unaware of.

Thank you deeply for spending both your time and money on this collection. I hope you've found as much pleasure and sweet pain in these stories as I enjoyed while writing them.

Jg
Portland, Oregon
April 2014

ABOUT JASON GURLEY

Jason Gurley is the author of the bestselling novel *Greatfall*, the post-Earth *Movement* series and *The Man Who Ended the World*, along with a number of short stories. His work has appeared in *From the Indie Side*, an anthology of speculative fiction edited by David Gatewood, and will appear in several more anthologies in 2014. He lives in Portland, Oregon, with his family, where he is currently writing *Eleanor*.

He can be found on Twitter (@jgurley) and at
www.jasongurley.com.